Angelica's Christmas Wish

Laina,
Blessings to you
in the New Year & always.
Carol Underhill
2019

Carol Underhill

ANGELICA'S CHRISTMAS WISH by CAROL UNDERHILL

ANAIAH ROMANCE
An imprint of ANAIAH PRESS, LLC.
7780 49th ST N. #129
Pinellas Park, FL 33781

First Anaiah Romance print edition November 2019

Edited by Kara Leigh Miller
Book Design by Laura Heritage
Cover Design by Laura Heritage

For my mom, Audrey Woolworth,
who always supported my desire to write.
She is celebrating with me from heaven.

ACKNOWLEDGEMENTS

Thank you to my late husband, Pat. You were my dream come true. "'Till death do us part" came too soon for us, but your love and faithfulness inspire me today.

I also want to thank my children, Travis, Holly, and Chad. You are my greatest blessings. Being your mom has given me the courage to face life's challenges and follow my dreams.

Thank you to my friends and family, for listening to me when I became discouraged and reminding me that God has a purpose for my life.

For all who have prayed for me on my writing journey and rejoiced in my good news, I can't wait to share my book with you.

Thank you to my editor, Kara Leigh Miller. You took a rough story and helped me create the book that I envisioned. I've learned so much through the editing process.

And most of all, I am thankful for my Heavenly Father for His goodness and faithfulness throughout my life.

CHAPTER ONE

ACCEPTING THE LEGAL-ASSISTANT JOB WAS an impulse. She'd sold everything, packed her clothes, and caught a bus to Chicago. She'd arrived last night, and already, she regretted the move.

Serena hunched forward as she tried to burrow deeper into her wool coat for protection against the biting wind. It was so much colder than she'd thought it would be, moving from North Carolina.

She'd thought her coat and boots were warm enough, but she hadn't counted on the cold wind around Lake Michigan. She had just purchased the boots she carried. She should have put them on instead of her leather boots, as they would have been better for walking through the slush on the sidewalks, but it was after noon, and she hadn't eaten lunch yet. She was in a hurry to get back to the hotel. Instead of sitting down in one of the restaurants in the shopping district, she would eat power bars and yogurt that she had brought with her.

Her employer had paid her moving expenses, but she had to pinch her pennies to afford the deposit and first month's rent on an apartment. The boots had been a costly purchase, but after only a day in Chicago, she'd realized she needed warmer ones.

Serena walked to a stoplight and stood on the corner, waiting for the light to turn. A little girl stood next to a woman who looked like she might be the grandmother. The child wore a knit hat that looked like a sock monkey. Her puffy coat and snowsuit were bright purple. She was splashing in the slush, impatiently waiting for the light to change. The woman held packages in both hands, and the little girl's hand was tucked in the older woman's pocket.

"Nana, do you think Santa will bring me my Christmas wish?"

"Angelica, you know Nana doesn't know what Santa will bring." The grandmother sounded like she had said it many times. "Why don't you tell me what you asked for?"

"If I tell you, it won't come true," the little girl said.

The grandmother caught Serena's eye, and

Serena smiled in sympathy. She knew firsthand how hard it was to get a child to tell a wish after sitting on Santa's lap.

She sighed. Christmas would be just another day this year. She was staying in a hotel for now, until she found an affordable apartment with a bus or train line to the downtown office where she would be working. Her new job was supposed to start the day after Christmas. She was ready for it. At least, she thought she was.

The light changed. The grandmother stepped off the sidewalk, with the little girl's hand still in her pocket.

"Look! There's Santa!" The child pointed at the figure across the street. She let go of her grandmother's coat and darted ahead. Tires screeched, and a car careened around the corner toward the little girl.

Serena's heart raced, and adrenaline surged through her. She dropped her packages and her purse and sprinted toward the car. She reached the girl before the car did and pushed her out of the way. Pain shot through her shoulder as the car slammed into her. Someone screamed. Then, she blacked out.

CHAPTER TWO

MARK SAT ACROSS FROM HIS CLIENT in the conference room. Her mascara ran down her cheeks as she sobbed. "My husband is just being spiteful. He wants me to have to go to work, even though I've never held a job in my life."

Mark reached across the table and patted her hand. Rings sparkled on every finger. The fake nails were painted deep red, matching the color of lipstick on her trembling lips.

"Mrs. Denton, I think your husband is being unreasonable, too. I don't think you should settle for his latest offer." He pulled his hand back as she lifted a lace hankie and blew her nose. "He can afford the amount of alimony we requested. And you shouldn't have to go to work at your age." She'd withheld her age, but he guessed late sixties.

Her eyes narrowed. "You're not just saying

4

that because you'll get more money if he pays more, are you?"

He sat back and folded his arms. "I've told you that my fee remains the same no matter how much alimony your husband pays. I want you to get what you deserve, since he's the one divorcing you after forty years of marriage."

Her eyes cleared, and she nodded. "Okay, then. Let's turn down his offer and see what happens."

The conference room door opened. His assistant, Shannon, stepped in and held out the phone. "Mark, I'm sorry to interrupt. It's your mother-in-law. There's been an accident with Angelica."

"An accident?" Mark's heart dropped. He grabbed the phone and jumped out of his chair. "Excuse me, Mrs. Denton. I need to take this call. Shannon, please phone for Mrs. Denton's driver and have him bring the car around. Mrs. Denton, I will talk to your husband's attorney and get back to you."

With a nod to his client, Mark left the conference room. He shook all over as he stepped into his office and shut the door. He lifted the phone to his ear. "Geneva, what happened?"

Geneva sobbed. "Oh, Mark! There was a car coming, and Angelica ran into the street. The car couldn't stop, and…"

Mark's heart threatened to pound out of his chest, and blood rushed in his ears. "Is she going to be okay?"

"She's—the ambulance is here now. They're checking her all over."

His daughter was crying in the background. His protective instincts kicked into high gear. "Tell me where you are, and I'll be right there."

"They're going to take her to the ER. I can go with her in the ambulance."

"You do that. I'll meet you at the hospital." Mark ended the call and tossed the phone onto his desk. His hands still shook as he grabbed his coat and threw his arms into the sleeves. He opened the door and rushed out. He couldn't lose his daughter! She was all he had in this world.

Shannon grabbed his arm as he raced through the reception area. "Mark, you have to calm down, or you'll have an accident on your way to the hospital yourself."

She was right. Mark straightened and put his arms at his sides, taking in a deep breath. As it whooshed out, his panicked thoughts slowed. "All right. Can you cancel my appointments? I'm going to be gone the rest of today. Maybe tomorrow, too. I don't know what I'm going to find when I get to the hospital—"

Shannon patted his arm. "I'll be praying for Angelica—and for you."

Mark grimaced. There'd been a time when he would have prayed in this situation, but the last time a tragedy had struck his family, prayer hadn't saved anyone.

He left the office and headed for the elevator. He hit the button several times, feeling panic rising again. It seemed like it took forever to ride the elevator to the main floor. He ran to the parking ramp where he'd left his car. He got in the car and took a moment to buckle his seat belt with trembling hands. As he drove out of the parking ramp, his tires screeched.

It was the noon hour, and the sidewalks were filled with pedestrians. He recalled in an instant that Angelica had been hit by a car driving too fast. He slowed as he entered the street. Traffic was thick. He drummed his fingers on the steering wheel, his thoughts racing ahead to what condition he would find his daughter in.

At the hospital, he parked in the lot for the emergency department. He hadn't been to the hospital for two years. Memories flooded his mind. He rested his head on the steering wheel, trying to find the strength he needed to walk in. Worry over Angelica overcame the grief, and he dashed into the lobby like a madman, out of breath.

The receptionist looked up, startled, as he pressed against the counter.

"Where is she? Where is Angelica Harper?"

"Mark?"

He followed his mother-in-law's voice. She'd been seated, but she stood and moved toward him. Her cheeks were tearstained, and her nose was red. He grasped her arms. "Is Angelica going to be all right?"

"I think so. She hit her head, but she was conscious. She chattered all the way to the hospital."

Mark let go of her arms and bent over, pressing his hands against his knees. Relief rushed through him. Angelica was conscious and talking. He straightened and took a deep breath.

"They think her arm is broken, but nothing else. They took her to X-ray, and I came out here to watch for you." Geneva started to cry. "I'm so sorry, Mark. I should have stopped her."

Mark patted her shoulder. His mother-in-law took care of Angelica every day without complaint. She would never let anything happen to her if she could help it. But she was seventy, and Angelica was an energetic five-year-old. Geneva didn't have an easy job trying to keep up with her.

"Let's go find out how she is."

Mark started toward the door to the emergency department. Geneva picked up the shopping bags she'd brought with her in the ambulance and followed Mark across the lobby.

The receptionist buzzed them through the door. A nurse at the desk inside the emergency department asked, "Who are you here to see?"

"Angelica Harper. I'm her father."

"Room three."

Mark tried to keep his cool as he walked past two empty rooms. In the third room, Angelica sat on the bed, holding her left arm across her chest. She appeared so small and fragile. His mind filled with relief that she was not badly injured.

Angelica looked up and smiled, although there were streaks down her cheeks where her tears had flowed. "Daddy!" She started to jump off the bed.

A nurse, who'd been standing to the side, moved quickly and stopped her from getting down. "Whoa there, girl. Let's not break your other arm."

Mark sat on the bed next to Angelica. He put his arm around her and gently squeezed her right shoulder. "I'm so glad you're okay, Ange." He brushed her hair back from her forehead, noticing a large lump that was already discoloring. "What happened?"

Her face crumpled. "I was bad, Daddy. I let go of Nana and ran into the street."

He hugged her, resting his cheek against her hair, damp with sweat. "You know better than that." His tone was gentle but firm.

She pulled away and tipped her head back. "I didn't mean to do it! Santa was standing on the corner, and I wanted to ask him if my Christmas wish was going to come true!"

That Christmas wish would be the death of him. It had nearly been the death of her. She still refused to tell him or her grandmother what she had wished for. "So, a car hit you?"

Angelica shook her head dramatically. "No, the car didn't hit me. It hit my guardian angel instead."

Mark turned to Geneva, who was seated by the window.

"There was a woman standing behind us. She ran after Angelica and pushed her out of the way. The car hit the woman instead."

Gratitude filled him as he thought of a stranger stepping in to save his daughter. Then, when he realized someone else had been injured because of his daughter's action, guilt weighed on him. "Is she okay?"

Before Geneva could answer, a doctor walked into the room. He put his hands on his hips. "You, my dear, are a very lucky little girl to come out of that accident with only a broken arm."

"My angel saved me."

Mark stood and shook the doctor's offered hand. "She seems a little confused. She thinks the woman who stepped in and rescued her is an angel." He shared a grin with the doctor.

Geneva put her hands on her hips. "Now, look, Mark. Angel, hero—whatever you want to call her—Angelica could have been hurt a lot worse if not for that woman."

The doctor walked to the bed. He gestured toward Angelica's arm. "You have two bones that run from your elbow to your wrist. You cracked them both." He turned to Mark. "It's a simple break. I'm going to set it and put a cast on. She'll need to follow up with an orthopedic doctor as soon as you can make an appointment. I don't want to wait on casting it. Her grandmother advised me that she's an active little girl."

Mark wasn't sure by the doctor's tone whether he should be proud or worried. "Yes, she is."

"So, let's get this arm in a cast."

The nurse went to a cabinet in the corner. She punched some numbers into a keypad, and the cabinet unlocked. She took a handful of colored packets out of a drawer, then held them out to Angelica. "We have four colors to choose from."

Angelica looked them over. "Don't you have any purple? Purple is my favorite."

"No purple." The nurse held up the red one. "How about this one? Red is a Christmas color."

Angelica's eyes sparkled. "Yes! That will match my dress for the program!"

The adults smiled at one another. Only a child

would be excited that her cast was going to match her dress.

It didn't take long for the doctor to wrap the arm. When he finished, he stood. He faced Angelica, but he spoke to Mark. "No gymnastics class until after she sees the orthopedic doctor." Angelica pouted. "No running or sledding or ice-skating. We don't want to injure that arm further." He shook his finger at Angelica and grinned. "You rest that arm, you hear? The only work I want you to do is open your presents on Christmas Day."

Angelica smiled, her dimples appearing. It was Lily's smile. Mark's chest tightened as he remembered his beautiful wife.

"You can wait in here until the nurse brings you the discharge papers to sign." The doctor and the nurse left the room.

It was another fifteen minutes before a different nurse brought in the paperwork. Mark scanned the discharge sheet and signed his name.

The nurse handed him the instruction sheet. "It says to rest the arm and give over-the-counter medication as needed. Follow up with an orthopedic doctor in a few days." She pressed her lips together. "Since it's so close to Christmas, you probably won't get in to see one until after the holidays. The recommended doctor is listed on the discharge instructions."

The nurse left. Geneva picked up the shopping

bags and Angelica's coat and snow pants. Her cheeks still had streaks of mascara on them, and her lips were pinched with worry. She looked tired.

"Let's just go with the coat for now," Mark said. He helped Angelica put her uninjured arm in the sleeve and buttoned it over the cast. He took the bags and snow pants from Geneva and led the way from the room.

As they started toward the exit, Angelica stopped. "I want to see my guardian angel and thank her."

Mark just wanted to get her home. "Let's come back and see her tomorrow."

Angelica stamped her foot. "No, I want to see her now."

He debated for a moment. Angelica was wound up from too much excitement. It had been a stressful day for her, the kind of day that led to tantrums. He sighed when he realized his daughter wasn't going to change her mind.

"Geneva, what do you think?"

"I would like to thank her. She did a heroic thing, running at that car and pushing Angelica out of the way." Geneva shuddered. "She was seriously injured. I think she was unconscious when they loaded her into the ambulance."

Mark wanted to somehow repay the woman who had saved Angelica's life, but his daughter was reaching the point of a meltdown. He held up the bags and snow pants. "Let's take these out to my car; then, we'll find some lunch."

"I'm starving!" Angelica said. "After we eat, we can come back, right?"

Maybe after Angelica had some food in her, she would be calmer. "All right."

She hugged him with her uninjured arm. He playfully tugged on the pom-pom at the top of her hat and then took her hand as they left the building.

CHAPTER THREE

A S THE PATIENT SLOWLY OPENED HER eyes, she became aware of a few things…

There was a sharp pain in her shoulder and ribs, along with a throbbing headache.

The lights were bright.

She was in a white room.

People were talking around her.

There were beeping noises.

Something squeezed her bicep, bringing her more fully awake. She glanced down at the blood pressure cuff. As the pressure released, she realized she was in a hospital.

How had she ended up here?

"Hello?" Her throat was dry; her voice hoarse. The chatter continued. "Hello?" she said again, a little louder.

The chatter stopped, and a face came into

view. As the patient focused, she saw a woman with a blond ponytail and wearing light blue scrubs.

"Oh, good. You're awake," the nurse said.

"Have I been asleep?"

"You've been unconscious since the ambulance brought you in. That was a couple of hours ago."

The patient blinked and looked around.

"How are you feeling?" the nurse asked.

"I hurt all over."

She received a look of sympathy from the nurse. "We can't give you anything for the pain until after you've seen the doctor."

"Why am I in a hospital?"

The nurse raised her eyebrows. "Don't you remember? You had an accident. You collided with a car."

That would explain why she was in pain. "I don't remember anything. How did the accident happen?"

The nurse rocked back on her heels. "I think I'd better get the doctor." She left the room.

The patient tried to sit up and clutched her abdomen as pain shot through her ribs. She lay back against the pillows, staring at the ceiling. Fear of the unknown made her feel helpless. Tears flowed out the corners of her eyes as she squeezed them shut and tried to remember what had happened to her.

The nurse came back with a doctor. "Hello there. I'm Dr. Schultz, the neurologist on staff." He walked closer to the bed. "We've performed an MRI, which came back with good news. There is no swelling or bleeding on the brain." He took an instrument from his pocket and shined light in her eyes. The bright light made her blink. He held up two fingers. "Follow my fingers with your eyes." He moved them up, then down, then to each side.

Trying to follow without moving made her head ache.

He brushed her hair from her forehead and touched a bump. "You're going to have a nasty bruise." He stood back. "Overall, you're very lucky. That car hit you pretty hard. Everyone is calling you a hero, though."

Her lip quivered, and she bit it. "Why are they calling me a hero?"

"You don't remember what happened?"

She shook her head, immediately regretting it as pain shot through her. "No. I only remember waking up here in this bed. I don't know how I got to the hospital."

He rubbed his chin and studied her. "You hit your head on the pavement. It's possible you have amnesia. Now, it's most likely temporary. You'll gain your memory back as your mind and body recover."

The thought of amnesia filled her with fear. She twisted the blanket. "How long will I have it?"

"Each case is different. Since there is no damage detected on the MRI, I believe it will come back to you quickly."

"And if it doesn't?"

He patted her shoulder. "Let's take this one step at a time. We're going to keep you overnight for observation. The nurse will administer some pain medication so you can rest."

Someone knocked on the door. They all turned and saw a police officer. "I came to take your statement, Miss."

Her heart pounded. She couldn't remember anything, and the police were involved. What was she going to do?

"She's not going to be able to give you one," the doctor said. "As of this moment, she doesn't remember the accident."

The officer folded his arms. His jaw moved back and forth as he studied the patient. "That makes things difficult. Should I come back later?"

"Why don't you call the desk first and make sure she's able to provide you with a statement? That will save you a trip."

"How long until she'll be able to do that?"

The doctor gestured for the police officer to leave the room and followed him out. The patient heard their low voices; then, they moved away from her room.

The nurse inserted medication into the patient's IV line. "This is something to help with the pain. It will probably make you sleepy, but that's okay. You need to rest."

When the nurse started to move away, the patient put out her hand and grasped the nurse's arm. "What kind of accident was I in?"

"Witnesses said the car came around the corner fast, and a little girl ran into the street. You ran after her and knocked her out of the way. The car hit you instead."

The patient gasped and covered her mouth with her hand. She'd run in front of a car to save a child? "What happened to the little girl? Is she going to be okay?"

"I heard that she was talking when the ambulance brought her in," the nurse said.

Well, that was some consolation. If the child had been talking, then she might not have been badly injured. "Will you let me know when you hear more about her?"

The nurse's features softened. She patted the patient's shoulder. "There are rules about what I can find out about a patient, but if I can, I'll let you know." The nurse lowered the bed and adjusted the pillows. "Now, try to get some rest. Maybe when you wake up, you'll remember."

"I hope so."

When the nurse left, the patient felt very much alone.

CHAPTER FOUR

After taking Angelica to her favorite downtown restaurant for lunch, Mark drove back to the hospital. He parked in the visitors' lot. He opened the back door for Angelica, but before she got out, he gave her some rules.

"The woman who saved you from getting hurt by the car is not a real angel. She's a human person, and she's injured. She may be in a lot of pain. I don't want you to be noisy and overwhelm her. Do you understand?"

Angelica nodded. "I'll be quiet. I promise."

Mark hid a grin as his gaze met Geneva's over the roof of the car. Angelica tried to keep her promises, but her exuberance often overruled her good intentions.

They walked into the main hospital entrance. This didn't affect Mark as much as it had earlier when he went through the emergency room doors. Lily hadn't been admitted to the hospital. She'd died in the emergency room, along with their premature infant.

He shoved his memories aside as he walked to the reception desk. The same woman who had been there earlier was sitting behind it. He gave her a polite smile. "I'm Mark Harper. I'm here to see the woman who was brought in earlier from the vehicle accident."

"I remember you. Are you her family?"

Mark grimaced. He knew the rules about not giving out patient information. "No, we're not her family. We would like to thank her for what she did for my daughter."

The receptionist pressed her lips together. "I'm unable to give out that information unless you're family."

Mark laid a hand on Angelica's shoulder. "I'm sorry, Ange. We'll have to find another way to thank her." He expected a temper tantrum, given that Angelica was tired and upset.

Instead, Angelica turned to the receptionist. "Please, can we see her? She's my guardian angel." She clasped her hands under her chin as if she were praying. It was the look she gave Mark or Geneva when she begged for something. He hid another grin. His daughter thrived on drama.

The receptionist's mouth twitched as her eyes

met Mark's. "She's irresistible, you know." She checked her computer screen. "She's on the second floor, room 226. But you didn't hear it from me."

Angelica hopped up and down. "Oh, thank you; thank you; thank you!"

Mark guided her away from the reception desk. Geneva lagged behind as they walked toward the elevators.

He slowed to wait for her and grew concerned at her pale face. On the way to the restaurant, she had wiped her mascara-stained cheeks and reapplied lipstick, but her efforts didn't hide the exhaustion in her eyes. "Are you feeling up to this?"

She drew her shoulders back and nodded. "I want to see and thank her."

They passed the gift shop on the way to the elevator. Angelica paused at the window. "Look at all those pretty flowers. We should buy some for her."

Judging by the expression on Geneva's face, she agreed. Mark rubbed the back of his neck. It didn't seem necessary to buy flowers.

"It wouldn't hurt to take her a bouquet," Geneva said.

Two against one wasn't fair. "Okay, then. Let Angelica pick something out." His patience wore thin while Angelica studied all the flower arrangements.

Angelica's shoulders slumped. "There aren't any purple ones."

"Purple isn't popular right now." Apparently, Geneva's patience hadn't worn thin. "It's almost Christmas. That's why most of the flowers are red and white, with holiday ribbons."

Angelica pointed to a bouquet of red and white carnations with a green ribbon that had Christmas trees on it. "This one."

It was up to Mark to carry the vase of flowers to the elevator as Geneva took Angelica's hand and carried her purse. He rode up silently, Angelica's chatter fading into the background as he thought about meeting this woman. He owed her a debt of gratitude, but taking flowers to her made him uncomfortable.

On the second floor, they walked to the nurses' station.

"Oh, hello," a bright young nurse said. "Can I help you?"

"We're here to see the woman who was hit by a car." Mark waited for her to ask whether he was family.

"Oh, good. She'll be so happy to see you."

He wondered at the enthusiasm but shrugged it off as the nurse led the way. She walked into the patient's room. "Your husband and daughter are here."

Mark jerked to a stop, nearly stumbling over

the nurse as she turned and left the room. Angelica raced ahead of him and stood beside the bed.

Mark set the vase on the shelf opposite the bed. He self-consciously met the patient's gaze. There was hope in her deep brown eyes.

"Are you—my husband and my daughter?"

He shook his head, and her lip quivered. "No, we aren't your family, I'm afraid."

"You're my angel!" Angelica's voice rose in excitement.

The patient's brow furrowed. "Angel?"

Mark pulled Angelica away from the bed. "I'm sorry."

"You saved my life," Angelica said.

Tears filled the patient's eyes. "I don't remember who I am."

Mark raised his eyebrows. "You have amnesia?"

She nodded, wincing. "The doctor said it's likely temporary." Her voice caught on the word *likely*.

He noticed the sling holding her left arm in place. Guilt tugged at him. She had taken the impact of the car so Angelica wouldn't get hurt. A broken arm wasn't a big deal compared with the head injury Angelica could have had. Instead, it was this woman who had the concussion. Now, she was in a hospital, not knowing who she was.

His throat felt tight. "You must have had an ID

on you—a purse, maybe?" His tone was sharp as he fought to hide his emotions.

Geneva tsked, and his face heated. His mother-in-law elbowed past him and walked to the bed. She took the patient's hand and patted it. "Remember," she said, frowning at Mark, "the police officer told us that her purse was stolen."

"So, no one knows who I am?" Tears ran down the patient's cheeks.

Geneva let go of her hand and reached toward the table, then pressed a tissue into the patient's hand. "You'll be all right, my dear," she said gently.

An older nurse walked into the room. "Are you all right? I thought you'd be happy now that your family is here."

"They aren't my family," the patient said.

Mark's face grew even warmer under the nurse's stare.

The nurse's eyes narrowed. "How did you get upstairs, then? They aren't supposed to let anyone in but family."

Mark didn't explain why the receptionist had given them permission. He drew Angelica to his side. "This is my daughter. Your patient saved her from getting hit by the car. We came to thank her."

"We brought her Christmas flowers!" Angelica ran over to the shelf and sniffed the bouquet.

Mark glanced at the patient. She twisted the tissue in her hands. The hope had gone out of her eyes, leaving only fear.

The nurse folded her arms. "You'll need to leave now. You're upsetting her."

Geneva patted the patient's shoulder. "We'll be praying for you, dear."

Mark straightened. Prayer wasn't an option with him. But he knew his mother-in-law well. She would offer prayers for the stranger.

"Okay. Let's go. Thank you again…" Mark hesitated, not knowing what to call the patient.

Her mouth curved slightly, but her smile didn't reach her eyes.

Mark took Angelica's hand as they walked out of the room. As they stood at the end of the hall, waiting for the elevator, she giggled. "She thought you were her husband and I was her little girl. Isn't that funny?"

Mark frowned. "It isn't funny, Angelica. It's sad that she doesn't remember who she is."

Out of the corner of his eye, he saw Geneva's smirk. "It is a little funny." She said it low enough that Angelica didn't hear.

He frowned. "She might be married, for all we know."

They rode the elevator down to the main floor. Angelica dragged her feet, unable to keep up with Mark. He stopped walking. "Are you all right,

Angelica?"

"My arm hurts."

Geneva leaned down and patted Angelica's shoulder. "Of course, it does. We've been so busy we haven't taken time to get any pain medicine."

They had just passed the gift shop. Mark looked over his shoulder. "Do you think they will have any in there?"

Geneva straightened. "I'll go in and check."

While Geneva went into the store, Mark picked Angelica up. "I'm sorry you're hurting, Angelica." At his gentle tone, Angelica rested her head in the crook of his neck. Her cast hit him in the chest. He could have lost her today. He leaned against the wall and laid his cheek against her hair.

"I'm sorry I was bad, Daddy. That lady got hurt because of me."

She was right about that last part, but she wasn't a bad kid. He didn't want her to carry the guilt over what she had done. "You weren't bad, Ange. You made a mistake is all."

Geneva came out with a small bag. "I got the medicine and a bottle of juice to wash it down with."

As Mark carried Angelica to the car, her cast kept bumping against his chest, a reminder of what she had been through. He opened the back door and buckled her into her booster seat. Geneva poured a dose of the liquid pain reliever and handed it to him.

Mark held it up to Angelica's lips. She swallowed and grimaced. He handed her the juice, and she drank half of it. After recapping the juice, he set it in the center console. He glanced back at her as he slid into the driver's seat. Her eyes were already closed.

He drove the few blocks to where Geneva had parked her car. By the time they reached it, Angelica was asleep. Geneva opened the passenger door and started to get out.

Mark stopped her with a hand on her elbow. "Do you think you could take Angelica home and get her into the house okay?"

Geneva's eyes widened. "Why? Aren't you going home?"

Mark shifted in the seat. "I thought I would go back to the hospital. I feel somehow responsible for her."

"For the woman who saved Angelica?"

Mark didn't like the twinkle in Geneva's eye.

He cleared his throat. "She thought I was her husband. Any man could show up there, pretending to be her husband, and convince her to leave with him."

"How will you be able to keep that from happening?"

Mark drummed his fingers on the steering wheel. He didn't know how he was going to protect the patient.

Geneva smiled. "She isn't wearing a wedding band."

It wasn't the first time Geneva thought of matchmaking. In recent months, she'd tried to set him up on dates with daughters of her friends from church. He'd refused to go out with any of them. He didn't want to get married again. Not after he'd lost the one woman he'd expected to spend the rest of his life with.

"Just take Angelica home, please." He used his lawyer voice.

Geneva huffed but didn't argue.

Mark and Geneva both got out of the car. Mark carried the sleeping Angelica to Geneva's car. Having a booster seat in each vehicle made things convenient. He buckled Angelica in while Geneva slid into the driver's seat.

Before Geneva could shut her door, Mark leaned down. "I'm not sure what time I'll be home."

"Do whatever you need to do for her, Mark. I don't like the idea of her being so vulnerable, either. It's good of you to care."

"I'm doing what anyone would do in these circumstances."

After Mark watched Geneva drive off with his sleeping daughter, he returned to his car. He hadn't looked at his phone all afternoon. He took it out now. He had messages from Shannon and the opposing attorney in the Denton case. He checked the time and called the attorney first. He got his voice mail.

"Hello, this is Mark Harper. I met with my client today. We both feel that your settlement proposal doesn't match my client's needs. Your client can afford to pay the amount of alimony we're asking for. Please suggest that he agree to our proposal so we can make the divorce final. Then, they can both move forward with their lives. I won't be in the office tomorrow, but you can reach me on my cell."

After ending the call, Mark checked the time. Shannon would have just left the office in the five o'clock traffic. He decided to call her later. Then, he headed back to the hospital. He'd wanted to thank the woman, but instead, he'd made her cry. He couldn't forgive himself for leaving her there in tears, even though the nurse had told them to go. He would make a quick visit to her room and express his gratitude properly. He might be able to investigate the accident a little and see whether there were any clues to her identity.

CHAPTER FIVE

THE PATIENT WOKE AND REALIZED SHE was still in a hospital bed. She tried to remember her name and the accident, but it was all a blank. Yet she could remember the doctor coming in. He had told her the amnesia was likely temporary. After the police officer had gone, a nurse had given her pain medication. She must have fallen asleep.

The bouquet of red and white carnations added color to the sterile white room. According to everyone, she had saved the little girl from getting hit by a car. It didn't sound like something she would do, but then, she couldn't remember anything about the person she'd been before waking up in the hospital. An image of the tall dark-haired man came to mind. She didn't think he meant to upset her. He'd obviously been uncomfortable at being presented as her husband.

There had been no mention of a wife, and she had no way of knowing whether she was married or even engaged. She was aware of the fact that her heart fluttered when she thought of him.

A nurse came into the room and stood beside the bed. "Oh, good. You're awake. How are you feeling?"

"I'm not in pain at the moment, but my memory hasn't come back."

The nurse patted her hand. "Try not to force your mind to remember. It will come back to you, I'm sure. Let's get you up; then, I will have a dinner tray brought in."

When the nurse raised the bed to a sitting position, pain rushed to the patient's head. The room felt like it was spinning. With the nurse's help, she managed to walk into the bathroom.

When she looked in the bathroom mirror, a stranger stared back at her. The dark brown hair and brown eyes weren't familiar to her at all. There were abrasions on her left cheek. She pushed back her bangs so she could see the lump on her forehead and the bruise forming around it. She touched it, wincing at the pain.

After she used the bathroom, the nurse helped her back into bed. By that time, her head was pounding. She leaned against the pillows and closed her eyes. Only when she heard someone's throat clearing did she open her eyes.

The man she'd thought was her husband stood in the doorframe. His dark eyes studied her. He walked forward a few steps. His smile was tentative. "How are you doing?"

She twisted the blanket in her hands. "I don't have my memory back yet. And no one has come looking for me."

He reached out and covered her hands. Warmth spread up her arm from the contact. He squeezed, then drew his hand back. "I'm sure they'll realize you're missing when you don't come home for supper."

"I hope so."

A nurse walked in with a steaming tray and set it on the bedside table. The man backed away, and the nurse dropped the bed rail. "Let's get you sitting up straighter." The nurse pressed the button with her foot, raising the head of the bed until the patient sat upright. "Is that all right?"

She shifted until she was comfortable. "That's good."

The nurse wheeled the table over until it was across her lap. The tray held a covered mug, a container of gelatin, and a small bottle of juice. With the way her stomach had been growling, it didn't look like much food.

"The doctor put you on a liquid diet for tonight to make sure your stomach won't get upset from the trauma or from the pain medication."

The nurse turned and left the room. "I really should leave," the man said. He started to step back and stalled, his gaze meeting hers.

He seemed reluctant to go. And she didn't want him to leave yet. His presence comforted her. "You don't have to go." She regretted her desperate words.

"I'll stay a little longer."

She struggled to get the lid of the mug off with one hand.

"Let me help you."

He lifted the lid and set it aside. Then, he opened the tea bag and dropped it into the water. She watched his hand as he swirled the tea bag around. He wasn't wearing a wedding band, but he had a daughter. Was he a single father?

He handed her the mug.

His kindness made her smile. "Thank you."

"Thank you. I owe you a debt of gratitude for what you did for my daughter."

She sipped her tea. She didn't care for the flavor, but the hot liquid was soothing. "I'm glad I was able to help, even if I don't remember doing so."

He opened the gelatin and juice for her. Then, he walked over to the window. He pushed the blinds aside and looked out. She wondered what he was thinking about.

A woman dressed in a sharp business suit

walked in, holding a cordless microphone. Behind her came a cameraman.

The man came to stand beside the bed as though guarding her. She felt safe with him there. "Can I help you?" His voice rang with authority.

"Yes, I'm from the local news station. I came to interview you. Someone from the accident scene got it all on video. Your brave action is going to be tonight's feature."

"If she gives you her permission, it will," the man said before the patient could.

He and the reporter had a stare down for a moment; then, she dropped the mike to her side. She stepped forward and held out her hand to the patient. "Hello, I'm Jessie. I'm a reporter, and I'd like to get the story on what happened to you." The patient shook her hand. "You're the woman who jumped in front of a car to save a little girl, aren't you?"

The patient's gaze went to the man. He seemed to be in control of the situation.

"You don't have to talk to them, if you don't want to," he said.

She shrugged. "I don't mind."

Jessie took a notepad and pen from her purse. "So, let's get some basic information first. What's your name?"

The patient gave a little laugh. "The interview is over."

"I beg your pardon?"

"I have amnesia. The doctor says it's likely temporary—"

The reporter leaned in closer. "Amnesia? That is quite the story. Maybe we can show your photo on TV and social media in case someone recognizes you."

The patient's gaze went to the man again. He faced the reporter. "I don't think that's a good idea. There are all kinds of crazy people in this city. What if someone comes in and lies and says he's her husband? She would just go with him, not knowing she was in danger."

The reporter's mouth dropped open. "Well, how can we help, then?"

"Go ahead and show the video feed of the incident. Do the same on social media. But don't use a close-up photo of her, and don't post any photos of my daughter, either."

"Your daughter?" The reporter's eyes nearly bugged out. "You're the father of the little girl she rescued? Do you two know each other?"

A flush started at his collar and rose into his face. "No. I never met her until today."

The reporter looked from his flushed face to the patient. "Now, there's a story right there."

"I'm here as her lawyer," he said.

The reporter stepped back. "All right, then. I guess we have no business here today."

He gave the reporter a pleasant smile. "You have live video. I'm sure that will capture your viewers' attention. But anything this woman said to you is off limits."

She gave a pointed nod toward the bed. "What does the patient say about it?"

The man turned his attention to the patient. "I'm sorry. I spoke for you. Do you want them to mention the amnesia?"

"I don't think so. I don't want any more crazies showing up, saying they're my husband." She grinned at him, and his eyes twinkled.

"So, there have been some, er, crazies show up?"

The patient shook her head. "No, I misspoke myself."

The reporter reluctantly left the room, and the cameraman followed her out. The man looked down at her. "So, I'm a crazy, huh?"

Even though she'd said it as a joke, she felt compelled to explain the misunderstanding. "I know that wasn't your fault. The EMTs who brought me in said that the little girl was my own daughter. Some of the nurses weren't aware that wasn't the case. So, when you showed up, they assumed, well, that you were my family."

"And the receptionist told us that no one was allowed up except family. We—Angelica, that is—convinced her to bend the rules."

She smiled at the affection in his voice. "Your daughter is very charming."

He grimaced. "She can be very persistent. But in this case, I'm glad she was. I wanted to tell you thanks for what you did, although a simple thank-you doesn't seem like enough."

She gestured toward the shelf, and he followed her gaze to the bouquet of flowers. "You have said thank you. And what you did for me tonight, with the reporter and everything, was very kind of you."

He cleared his throat. "Since you don't know who your family members are, I want you to take my card." He reached into his pocket and brought out a business card. He took a pen from the same pocket, scrawled a number on the back, and handed the card to her.

"Mark A. Harper, attorney at law," she read. She lifted wide eyes to him. "You really are an attorney."

"Yes. And if you need anything, I want you to give me a call. If you don't want to talk to anyone about what happened, don't feel like you're obligated to. You can check with me first."

She laid the card on the table beside her tray of food that had grown cold. "Thank you for watching out for me."

He patted her shoulder. "My pleasure. Because of your heroic act, my daughter has only a broken arm and a bump on her head. She could have been gravely injured." He turned and left the room.

She watched him go, wondering at the way he stirred her heart.

CHAPTER SIX

A S MARK DROVE HOME FROM THE hospital, he tried not to think about the stranger. He told himself that he was just looking out for her, as he would for anyone. Why, then, did the memory of her soft brown eyes stick with him? She had teased him about being a crazy, and the smile she gave him tripped his heart. When he got closer to home, he switched his focus to Angelica. Since Geneva hadn't called, Mark guessed his daughter had settled in well after her hectic day.

When he got home, Angelica didn't greet him at the front door as usual. He walked in, hung up his coat, and removed his shoes. He followed the voices to the kitchen. His daughter and mother-in-law were seated at the table. They had a board game in front of them. Angelica's head was propped on her elbow.

"Daddy, you're home!" She didn't get up and hug him, as she normally would.

He walked over and hugged her. He pushed her bangs back and studied the lump and the bruise that had formed around it. He gently kissed a spot beside it. "How are you doing, Ange?"

"I'm tired, and my arm hurts."

Mark glanced at Geneva for confirmation. "She can't have another dose of medicine for a half hour yet," she said.

He straightened and looked around. Usually, Geneva kept supper warm for him when he was late.

"I put the soup in the fridge. Would you like me to heat up a bowl for you?"

"No, that's okay." Mark gestured for her to remain seated. "I'll warm it up in the microwave."

"I wasn't sure what time you'd be home."

"I stayed for a while. I'm glad I did. The news team showed up and wanted to interview her. I told them I was her lawyer so they would be cautious in what they broadcast."

Geneva's mouth curled, and her eyes twinkled as they met his. "It's good she has you watching out for her."

He ignored the underlying message. He took the soup from the fridge, ladled it into a bowl, and set it in the microwave. Then, he leaned against the counter and glanced around the room. He recalled the way the kitchen had looked before Lily redecorated it. When Lily's father passed away, he left debt that would have forced Geneva to sell Lily's childhood home and get a job in her sixties. Her home was in one of the best school districts in Chicago. Mark and Lily moved in with Geneva and paid the household expenses, while she provided childcare for Angelica.

Before they moved in, Lily had asked her mother whether she could renovate the house. Geneva had given her free rein to make any changes she wanted to. Lily worked with a designer to transform the outdated country-charm style she'd grown up with into sleek modern. Lily's touch was everywhere.

The microwave dinged. Mark stirred the soup and checked the temperature. He buttered a couple of Geneva's homemade rolls and took a seat at the table. He watched the board game while he ate. "Who's winning?"

"I am," Angelica said. "Did you talk to my angel?"

"I talked to the woman who saved you, yes. No one has showed up looking for her yet."

"We can bring her home with us."

Mark choked on his spoonful of soup. "No, we can't, Ange. She has a home to go to." To avoid any further questions, he pushed his empty bowl aside. "Can I get in on this game?"

"We're done with this round." Geneva stood. "Why don't the two of you play one game; then, we'll put it away. I think Angelica should have an early bedtime tonight."

"Nana!" Angelica looked at him. "Daddy, do I have to?"

It was one of Angelica's favorite tricks. If Nana told her no, she would ask him. After Lily died, he had been numb and unable to cope with Angelica's requests. She'd learned quickly that he would say yes when he wasn't paying attention to what she'd asked, even if Geneva had already told her no. It didn't take long for Geneva to call him out on it. Figuring she knew what was best for his daughter, more than he did at the time, he'd agreed to check with Geneva before promising anything. He'd overcome the numbness and was more involved in the daily decisions, but he and Geneva still put up a united front. When they disagreed, they talked it over privately. It worked for them.

"Early bedtime, I agree," Mark said. Angelica pouted.

Geneva poured a dose of medicine into a cup. "Here you go, sweetie."

Angelica frowned but swallowed the medicine, followed by a drink of juice.

Mark shuffled the cards and placed them on the board. "What color do you want me to be?"

"You take blue. I'm using red to match my cast."

Angelica won the game, with a little help from Mark. He wanted to end her day on a good note. He boxed up the board and pieces. She yawned. "Ready for bed, Ange?"

"I guess."

Following their usual routine, Mark helped her put on her pajamas. It was difficult. They chose a loose-fitted T-shirt that she could get on over her cast. Then, she curled up on his lap on the sofa while he read to her. Geneva sat across from them in her recliner. Usually, she drank a cup of tea and read in the evenings. Tonight, she tipped her head back against the cushion and closed her eyes. He realized that she'd had a very exhausting, stressful day.

Angelica fell asleep while Mark read the story. He held her after he put the book down, more to comfort himself than her. He could have lost her today. He'd already lost Lily. If he hadn't had Angelica to live for, he didn't know what he would have done in the months after Lily passed away. Mark carried Angelica into her bedroom and tucked her in.

When he returned to the living room, he touched Geneva's shoulder.

She woke up, startled. "Oh, I guess I dozed off."

"Would you like me to make you a cup of tea?"

"No, I don't think so, Mark. Thank you for offering." She yawned and stretched as she stood. "I'm going to turn in early myself."

After Geneva went to bed, Mark decided to return Shannon's call. He'd asked Shannon to cancel tomorrow's appointments, and he wanted to know whether anything new had come up today that needed his attention tomorrow.

As he dialed Shannon's number and waited for her to answer, he thought about the fact that he was going to lose the best assistant ever. He wasn't even sure what Shannon did to keep the law firm running as smoothly as it did. He'd let Shannon place the ad for a new assistant and left the interviewing and hiring up to her, too. His new assistant was scheduled to begin the day after Christmas. Shannon planned to stay until New Year's to train her replacement. Hopefully, the new assistant would meet Mark's expectations.

"Hi, Boss," Shannon answered.

Mark smiled. He would miss their easy camaraderie. "I thought I would let you know that Angelica is going to be all right. She has a broken arm but otherwise is uninjured."

"How's her guardian angel doing?"

Mark groaned. "Angelica called you already, didn't she?"

Shannon giggled. "You did give her my cell

phone for emergencies. I was quite surprised to get a call from her earlier this evening telling me about her angel."

"Yeah, well. I don't believe in guardian angels, you know."

"Oh, I know." She was laughing outright now. "But your daughter and your mother-in-law do. Has the woman figured out who she is yet?" she asked in a serious tone.

"She hadn't learned anything about her identity before I left. I'll call and check on her again in the morning. Are all of my appointments for tomorrow rescheduled?"

"Yes, I called the clients and set up new appointments for after Christmas."

"That will give me tomorrow to make sure she's all right."

"Angelica? Or the woman?"

Mark cleared his throat. He was reluctant to admit he was thinking about the woman in the hospital, not his daughter. Some kind of father he was, right?

"So, what's this all about? Are you her guardian angel now? Geneva said she isn't wearing a wedding band, nor does it look like she has worn one recently."

"That's neither here nor there," he said defensively.

"Uh-huh. This is the first time you've paid

attention to a woman since Lily died."

"I feel responsible for her since she rescued Angelica. Nothing more." He ignored the little voice that called him a liar.

"Mark, God works—"

He clenched his jaw. "Don't say it, Shannon. I don't want to hear how God works in mysterious ways. I get enough of that from Geneva."

"I won't mention it again, but you already know what I believe."

"I'll keep you informed," he said, then ended the call. He didn't say he used to believe that God worked all things out for the good, before the premature labor and the fight to save Lily and the baby. All those verses he'd memorized now seemed to be myths. He still believed in a higher power, but no longer did he feel that God was always good.

Mark tried to get interested in one of his favorite TV crime dramas, but it was hard to focus on it tonight. He kept replaying the day. The call from Geneva, the mad rush to the hospital, the relief when he saw Angelica had not suffered serious injury. His thoughts drifted to the woman he'd met. He tried to figure out ways to help her find her relatives, without bringing unwanted media attention. He selfishly wondered whether she was married or engaged or in a steady relationship. Somehow, if he found out she was, it would be disappointing. It bothered him that he cared.

At eleven o'clock, he turned on the local news. The top story was the accident. A bystander had taken video. His heart stopped when he saw the car come flying at his daughter. He watched as the woman sprinted, leaped in front of Angelica, and pushed her out of the way. There was no question it was a heroic act. She had put her life on the line for his daughter. It was no wonder that Angelica called her a guardian angel.

CHAPTER SEVEN

MARK'S CELL PHONE RANG WHEN IT felt like he had just closed his eyes. The time on his phone read three thirty. It was an unknown number, but he answered it anyway. "This is Mark Harper."

"You told me I could call if I needed something."

It was the woman from the hospital. Mark sat upright, wide awake. "Are you all right?"

"No one came for me. I'm still in the hospital."

"Has your memory come back yet?"

"No, I thought someone would come for me by now." Her voice was reaching panic level.

"I'll come. I should be there in twenty minutes." He set his phone down. He pulled on jeans and a sweatshirt, then went into Geneva's room and gently shook her.

She rolled over and blinked as her eyes tried to focus on him without her glasses.

"The woman from the accident called me. She's still at the hospital. I'm going to go and see what she needs."

Geneva glanced at her clock. "At this hour?"

"I told her to call if she needed me. She's scared and alone."

"Go, then. Lock the door when you leave."

Mark took the quickest route to the hospital. The visitor entrance was locked, so he went through the door of the emergency room.

"Can I help you?" the woman behind the desk asked.

"I'm here to see a patient. I know it's not visiting hours, but she called me, and she—needs me."

"What's her name?"

"It's the woman with amnesia who was brought in earlier today."

"I heard about that. Go on up. I'll buzz the nurses' station so they're expecting you."

Mark's heart pounded as he rode the elevator. What was he doing in the middle of the night, answering a stranger's call for help? The idea that she had woken up alone and frightened had him racing here to be with her. But was it a good decision?

When he walked off the elevator, a nurse stood

waiting for him.

"I'm Mark Harper."

"They called from downstairs and told us you were coming. It's unusual to have a visitor at this hour, but the patient said she called you. Go ahead and see what she needs."

Mark walked down the hall toward the patient's room. Perspiration dampened his palms. He rubbed them on his jeans, then took a deep breath before entering the room. She'd been crying, and her eyes were puffy. Her gently sloped nose was red. Yet she was even prettier than he remembered.

"I'm sorry I bothered you."

"You aren't bothering me. I'm glad you called. I've been worried about you."

"I'm so scared. I don't know what to do." Tears rolled down her cheeks. "I thought someone would come by now."

"Maybe they don't know where to look."

She brushed away her tears.

Mark handed her a tissue. "You have an accent. Did you know that?"

"What kind of accent?"

"A southern accent. You're not originally from Chicago."

Her brow furrowed. "What am I doing here, then?"

He shrugged. "I don't know. I'm sure someone

is looking for you."

"Are you sure?"

At the hope in her voice, he wanted to be sure. Instead, he squeezed her hand. With his other hand, he brushed her hair back from her forehead. She flinched as he touched her bruise. "Sorry. It looks very painful." He dropped his hands to his sides. "I saw videos of the accident on the news last night. What you did was very brave."

She dipped her chin and blushed, as if she wasn't used to receiving compliments. "I don't feel like I'm a very brave person."

"Maybe it was an adrenaline rush. I've heard that people can be very heroic in desperate circumstances. You saw a child in danger and responded. You didn't even think about the fact that you were putting yourself in danger." The fact that it was his child she had risked her life for made him admire her more.

Head lowered, she focused on a snag in the thermal blanket. She stuck her finger through the looped thread and toyed with it.

Mark sat in the vinyl recliner. It looked like he might be here awhile. He should be home in bed, sound asleep. Instead, he was keeping a frightened stranger company.

She pushed the snag away and shifted so she could look at him easier. "I don't remember what your daughter's name is."

"Angelica. Angelica Eve, the Eve after my mom."

She smiled. "That's a pretty name. Was that your mom here with you?"

"No, my mother-in-law."

"Oh." Her mouth fell open. "You're married?"

Why it mattered to her, he wasn't sure. He guessed she would have felt uncomfortable spending these early hours of the morning in the company of a married man. "I'm widowed. My wife passed away two years ago."

She bit her lip. "I understand."

The way she said it, with sympathy, made him wonder how well she understood his being widowed. "You don't have a wedding ring on. Maybe you're a widow, too?"

She looked at her left hand. "I don't know if I was ever married."

"You'll figure everything out." Why her marital status mattered to him, he was unequally sure. He didn't intend to marry again and had rejected the idea of dating. Yet he couldn't deny feeling a connection to her.

He watched as she looped the snagged thread around her finger again. She played with it for a moment, then let go. She folded her hands. When she looked back at him, her dark eyes reflected calm.

"Tell me about your daughter."

His favorite topic. He sat back against the vinyl cushion and crossed his ankle over his knee. "She's five years old. Just started kindergarten this year. She is off school for the Christmas holiday."

Her eyes widened. "It's Christmas?"

"In three days. Well, two, really. This is Friday morning. Tomorrow is Christmas Eve."

"Oh, I hope I'm out of here by Christmas. Although, I don't think I have anywhere to go." Her lower lip quivered.

He upped his efforts to distract her from her fears. "My daughter was born on Christmas Day. That's why we named her Angelica, like a Christmas angel. She's always so excited and says she gets double presents because it's both her birthday and Christmas."

She raised an eyebrow. "Does she get double presents?"

He gave her a sheepish grin. "She is pretty spoiled, I would say. Especially since her mom has been gone. My wife was more practical. I have a hard time saying no to her."

"I can imagine. She's very cute."

Hearing the compliment warmed his heart. Angelica was his whole life. "I'm afraid she's also very clever. This year, she wouldn't tell me what her Christmas wish was. We—my mother-in-law and I—are hoping we guessed right on what she wanted."

A far-off look came into her eyes. "She sounds like a little girl I used to know."

He leaned forward, all amusement gone. "You remember a little girl?"

She gave her head a shake, and her eyes cleared. "No, not really. I don't know why I said that."

"See—maybe your memory is coming back."

A nurse came into the room. "How are you doing, Miss?"

"I'm okay. I'm getting pretty sleepy, though."

"That's to be expected. When you woke up, we gave you a sedative to relax you. You were anxious and in pain."

"I'm feeling better now." The patient smiled at Mark.

He felt himself blushing at the knowing look the nurse gave him.

The nurse turned back to the patient. "We gave you the medicine a couple of hours ago. You should try and go to sleep now. The doctor will examine you when he makes his rounds. He'll probably let you go home today."

She sat upright, looking panicked. "I don't know where my home is."

The nurse patted her shoulder. "I'm sure we'll find someplace for you to go."

She lay back down, and the nurse left the room.

Mark stood and put his hands on the bed rail. "I should go, too." He didn't miss the disappointment in her eyes. He shouldn't let it affect him. "I'll check back on you later."

She gave a small smile. "Okay."

Outside the room, Mark caught up to the nurse in the hallway. "You can't discharge her when she doesn't know who she is or where she is supposed to go."

"I don't make the decisions," the nurse said. "I don't think they're going to keep her another night."

Mark was frustrated, but he didn't want to take that out on the nurse. As she'd pointed out, it wasn't up to her whether the patient was discharged. Perhaps he could show up around the same time as the doctor and express his concerns then.

As Mark rode the elevator to the main floor, he thought about the fact that he should go home and not worry about what would happen to the woman who saved his daughter's life. Yet a sense of responsibility for her stubbornly persisted, against his better judgment. He tried to tell himself he would feel this protective about anyone in her circumstances.

But her dark brown eyes had drawn him in. They were so expressive. Her fear had diminished as they talked. She was very beautiful. He sighed.

He should not be noticing how beautiful she was. She was in a vulnerable position. And he was not responsible for her.

Yet he considered her accent, which might mean she'd only recently come to Chicago. Was it possible she had no friends or relatives looking for her? He glanced at his phone as he stepped off the elevator. It was six o'clock. Angelica was an early riser and would be awake by now. He needed to get his priorities straight and put his daughter first.

The lobby wasn't crowded, but there were enough people around that he didn't want to make the call to Geneva there. Instead, he went outside and sat on a bench near the circle drive. People came and went through the hospital doors, but he was far enough away that he would not be overheard.

Geneva answered on the first ring. "Hello, Mark."

"How is Angelica this morning?"

"Her arm hurts, and so does the bump on her head. I gave her some pain medicine with her breakfast."

"At least she slept through the night," Mark said.

Geneva sighed with relief. "Yes, and she seems wide awake this morning as usual. So, that's a good sign. Are you going into the office?"

"No, I had Shannon clear my calendar for

today." He waited for her reaction.

"Oh?" Her voice rose with surprise. "I thought with Angelica being okay, you would go to work today. Are you coming home, then?"

"I think I'll stick around the hospital until the doctor comes in." He tried to keep his tone casual, but she wasn't a fool.

"You're getting awfully involved." Instead of sounding upset, Geneva sounded delighted.

Mark cringed at the impression he was giving her. Unfortunately, she wasn't wrong. He was getting more involved with the patient than he ought to. "The nurse said she would likely be discharged today, but she doesn't remember who she is or where she lives."

"Where will she go?"

He switched his phone to the other ear. He'd been wondering that same thing. "Maybe to a hotel? Or a women's shelter?"

Geneva tsked. "You're not going to let them turn her out on her own, are you?"

His conscience would never allow him to abandon this stranger, not in a big city like Chicago. But he could follow through and check on her, make sure she was settled in somewhere while she waited for her memory to return.

"You could bring her here."

Had he heard his mother-in-law right? "What did you say?"

"You can bring her here," Geneva repeated, "to stay with us until she recovers."

It was a crazy idea. "She's a stranger. We're strangers to her. I can't do that. She'll get the wrong idea." There was physical attraction between them. If he brought her home, would he give her the impression he was interested in her as more than a stranger who'd saved his daughter's life?

"What idea could she possibly have?" Geneva asked, teasing in her tone.

He didn't tell her he'd spent nearly two hours holding the stranger's hand and talking with her to comfort her. Or how attractive he found her, with her big dark eyes and long, thick lashes. He couldn't follow through on the attraction he felt. What if she regained her memory and realized she wasn't single, despite not having a ring? "I'm sure someone is looking for her."

"You can leave your name and number with the police station, and the hospital has it, too. If someone comes looking for her, they'll know where to reach her."

"I suppose so."

"It's the Christian thing to do, Mark."

"That may be, but you know how I feel about that right now."

"I wish you would look to your faith again. You were so close to the Lord before. It's a shame to see your belief in God's love fade."

His faith in God's love ended when Lily and the baby died. He'd barely moved past his grief, and then, he'd almost lost Angelica yesterday. It was the stranger's intervention that had saved his daughter. He didn't feel like he owed God any thanks. Even as those thoughts entered his mind, guilt stirred in his heart.

"Ask her if she wants to come home with us until she finds where she belongs," Geneva suggested. "At least, she won't have to spend Christmas alone somewhere."

He sighed. His mother-in-law had made up her mind. "If they discharge her today, I'll ask her if she wants to come to our house."

"Now that it's settled, should I get some things for her to wear?"

Mark hadn't thought of that. The woman was wearing a hospital gown. She would have the clothes she was brought in somewhere, but they might be dirty from falling on the pavement. "I suppose it wouldn't hurt."

"I think she is about the same size as Lily, isn't she?"

"How would I know?" He didn't like the implication that the stranger was like his wife. In sizes, though, they were similar. He shouldn't have noticed, but he was a guy who had been alone for a while. And she was pretty. "Yes, she's about the same size as Lily."

He could picture his mother-in-law's smug look. "Okay, then. I'll pick up some things that might work, some leggings and sweaters." Her tone reflected her amusement.

Mark tried to derail his mother-in-law's matchmaking. "Don't go to much trouble. Someone is bound to find out where she is. She won't need much."

"Where's your Christmas spirit, Mark?"

His throat felt tight. "Did you ever find out what Angelica's wish was?"

"She wouldn't tell me."

Mark sighed. "I don't want Angelica to be disappointed if we guessed wrong."

"That's spoiling her, you know. Getting her whatever she wants when she wants it."

That had been Lily's opinion, too, and it had always been an argument between them. He'd wanted to give Angelica the world, and Lily had wanted her to stay grounded. Lily was raised with money, while Mark grew up with parents who lived paycheck to paycheck. He worked hard to get good grades in high school and received a scholarship to University of Michigan, where he'd met Lily. She'd been a sorority pledge, and he'd been a poor student who worked two jobs to pay for what the scholarship didn't cover. But they'd hit it off, and both were studying to be lawyers.

Their financial status had evened out when they'd gotten married after law school and found jobs as associates in downtown Chicago at different firms. They worked long hours those first few years as they started up the ladder toward making partner.

Lily's climb halted when she gave birth to Angelica. She'd decided she wanted a job with less stress, so she opened a private practice where she could set her hours.

Geneva cleared her throat, and Mark's mind came back to the present.

"We'll talk about all of this later." He ended the call and pocketed his phone. His early-morning trip to the hospital was catching up to him. His mother-in-law had picked up on his concern for the patient and turned it into something more than it was. He hadn't meant to get frustrated with Geneva.

Maybe he would be better able to deal with the situation once he had some caffeine and breakfast. He went to the cafeteria and ordered a coffee and a bagel. A newspaper lay on the counter, so he took it to the booth with him. The accident had made the front page, but it wasn't the top story. The details were pretty much the same as given in the news broadcast—except the reporter had spoken with the police and the woman was hospitalized and, as of the time of press, unidentified. At least, that was better than having it broadcast all over social media that she had amnesia. Not every crazy person read the morning news.

He grinned as he remembered her joking that he was a crazy person. The reporter had questioned her, and she'd said she misspoke. But he knew she'd been teasing him. How was it possible to develop such a connection when she didn't even know her name?

Geneva had given him an idea. She'd mentioned leaving his number with the police. He could use his connections to both help her and protect her.

He used his cell to look up the number for the police station. There wasn't anyone around him in the cafeteria, but it was a conversation he didn't want overheard. He tossed the unfinished portion of his bagel and, taking his coffee, left the cafeteria and walked outside. He punched in the number. When someone answered, he introduced himself as the patient's attorney, even though she hadn't retained him. That got him through to the police chief right away.

"How can I help you, Mr. Harper?"

"I'm representing the woman who was hit by a car yesterday. Are you the person who spoke to the news reporter?" Mark used his lawyer voice, as Shannon jokingly called it. In general conversation, he spoke rather quietly. But when he was on the job, he spoke louder and with an authoritative tone meant to intimidate. It also boosted his confidence when he was stepping into new territory, like this phone call.

"Yes. I only gave information about the case that I am allowed to say." The police chief sounded defensive.

"Do you have any leads on her identity?" Mark toned down the volume a little. No sense making an enemy of the police chief.

"I haven't had anyone call in to file a missing person's report. We've checked with other local stations, and no one else has heard anything, either." The defensiveness dropped, and concern filled the police chief's voice. "It's a shame that she has amnesia."

"I agree." Mark took a sip of his coffee. "What happened to the driver who hit her?"

"He was under the influence of a controlled substance. We arrested him, and he'll be arraigned later this morning."

Mark felt some satisfaction in hearing that the driver was going to be charged. But that didn't help the patient. "If you get any leads on her identity, you can call me on my cell." He left his number. He put his phone away, satisfied that he had made the best effort he could to help. He really should just walk away at this point. He didn't want to encourage her to depend on him, but his conscience wouldn't let him do that, especially now that Geneva was involved.

Instead of going home, he headed back upstairs to see the patient. As he stepped off the elevator, a scream tore through the quiet atmosphere.

CHAPTER EIGHT

THE PATIENT WOKE UP SWEATING, HEART pounding, with tears rolling down her cheeks. She'd had a nightmare of a car crash, a little girl's screams and blood.

When she opened her eyes and became aware of her surroundings, someone was calling her "Miss." A nurse leaned over her. "You were screaming. You must have been having a nightmare."

"I think so."

Her gaze flitted around the room and landed on the tall, handsome man who had held her hand this morning. What was his name?

Mark. That was it.

He stepped up to the bed. "Were you dreaming about the accident?"

"I remember a car crash. A little girl

screaming. And blood everywhere."

His eyebrows drew together. "There was no blood involved."

"But it seemed so real."

Her hair clung to her forehead, damp from her sweat. Mark brushed it back, avoiding the tender lump. When his touch lingered, calm settled over her, easing the anxiety her nightmare had caused.

A doctor walked into the room with a jovial grin. "How is our superhero today?"

The patient's cheeks grew warm at the admiration in the doctor's eyes. Her gaze shifted to Mark, and she saw admiration in his as well.

"You are definitely my hero." His voice was low and felt like a caress. "I'll check back with you later."

When Mark turned to leave, the doctor reached out and stopped him. "You might as well stay so I can talk to the both of you at once, if that's okay with our patient."

The doctor seemed to assume that Mark was related to her. She didn't tell him any differently, wanting Mark to stay. His presence settled her nerves.

"He can stay."

The doctor walked up to the bed. "How are you feeling this morning? Are you in any pain?"

"Not really."

"I gave her pain medicine a couple of hours

ago," the nurse said.

"How about your memory? Has it come back at all?"

She told him about the nightmare. "But Mark says that the accident wasn't like the one in my dream. There was no blood yesterday, he said."

The doctor looked at Mark. He nodded, tight lipped.

"A nightmare isn't unusual given the trauma you went through yesterday. From a medical standpoint, you're ready to go home."

She gave a laugh that bordered on hysterical. "I don't have any place to go."

"Oh, I thought…" The doctor's eyebrows rose as he looked at Mark. "You're not her husband?"

A flush went up from Mark's neck to the tips of his ears. It was the second time he had been mistaken for her husband. Obviously, he was embarrassed. "No, I'm the father of the little girl she saved from the car accident."

"And you are here because—"

"He came because I called him. I was frightened because no one has come forward who knows me yet. He's been very kind to me."

Mark's gaze met hers, and the kindness that she spoke of radiated from his dark eyes.

"In that case, we need to find somewhere for you to go. A shelter, maybe."

Tears filled her eyes. She didn't want to be

released to go to a strange place where she knew no one.

"How can you release her when she doesn't know who she is?" Mark asked. "And her memory of the accident isn't accurate."

Her chest expanded with gratitude for his protection. "Mark is also here as my lawyer."

Mark offered his hand, and the doctor shook it. "Mark Harper, attorney at law. I'm here in an unofficial capacity, but I promised our patient I would see that she is safe."

The doctor leaned back and crossed his arms. He tapped his foot as he mulled over Mark's words. "Well, in that case, what do you suggest we do?"

"I can take responsibility for her release. She can come to my house until her memory recovers."

"But I don't know you," she said.

"You've met my mother-in-law. She lives with me. Or rather, I live with her. And my daughter thinks you're her guardian angel. I have to admit, she has me almost believing it, too. You're my hero."

She blushed. "I'm not a hero. I did what anyone would do if they had a chance."

While it was a generous offer, she didn't know him at all. Why, he could be a monster—no, the gentleness in his expression warmed her heart. He was a caring man. Every instinct told her she could trust him, and right now, what other options did she have? She looked at the doctor to see what he thought.

"I think you should take Mr. Harper up on his offer. You shouldn't be on your own. You need someone to help you, with your arm in the sling, and to watch over you when you're on the pain medication. Besides that, until you get your memory back, you're in a vulnerable position."

Tears spilled onto her cheeks. Where were her family and friends? Did she have no one who cared about her?

Mark stepped forward and put his hand on her shoulder. "What do you say? Do you want to go home with my family and let us watch out for you?"

"What if I don't get my memory back?"

"We'll figure it out."

"All right, then. I'll go to your house. With your mother-in-law and daughter." Emphasizing their presence made her feel more secure in her decision.

Mark squeezed her shoulder, then stepped back. He faced the doctor.

"Mr. Harper, since you're not related, you'll both need to sign some release forms. I'll have a nurse bring them right in." The doctor turned and left the room.

She twisted her hands in her lap. "I'm sorry to

be a bother."

"You're not a bother," came a cheery voice from the doorway. She saw the woman and child from yesterday.

The little girl rushed over to the bed. Mark put his hand on her shoulder, slowing her.

"You're coming home with us!" she said.

She was suddenly overwhelmed by the idea of going home with strangers. None of her other options were appealing, but this was a family. She didn't belong with them. She wished she could stay here in the hospital another night or until someone identified her.

She brought a shaky hand up to her forehead. "I'm not sure I should."

"Oh, please?" Angelica's little face scrunched up. "I want to spend Christmas with my guardian angel."

"Sweetie, I'm not an angel. I'm a real person. A human."

"So? You saved my life. We get to spend Christmas with you." Angelica would not be deterred.

Mark frowned at Angelica. Then, he turned back to the patient. "I'm sorry. Once Angelica gets something in her head, it's hard to change her mind."

"Impossible, you mean." The older woman walked to the bed. "I'm Geneva, Angelica's grandmother. I don't know if you remember me from yesterday. I was there when you rushed into the street and pushed Angelica out of the way of that car." Her words faltered, and tears filled her eyes. She blinked them back and smiled. "It was very brave of you. That's why she's so excited and calling you her guardian angel."

"But she's not—" Mark started to argue.

Geneva's stern look interrupted his protest. "Angelica and I feel that God sent you to save her from serious injury."

The patient wasn't sure what she felt about God, but it was obvious from Mark's frown that he didn't agree with his mother-in-law.

He lifted his hands in surrender. He leaned toward her and said in a stage whisper, "Would you feel comfortable with these two"—he nodded toward his daughter and Geneva—"lunatics?"

She giggled, but she was the only one amused.

Angelica said, "Daddy!" and Geneva tsked.

"I guess, if you're sure it will be all right, then yes, I will go home with you. I don't have many choices right now."

He straightened, and his expression turned serious. "I've left my number with the police station, and I'll also give it to the hospital administration, so if someone is looking for you—" His gaze met hers. Her fear must have been obvious because he gave her a gentle smile. "*When* someone is asking about you, they'll know where you are. And that you're safe."

"Now, shoo, Mark, while she gets dressed." Geneva held up a canvas shopping bag. "I've brought some clothes for you, Miss—" She put her hands on her hips. "Now, whatever are we going to call you? We can't keep referring to you as Miss. Why, you might even be married, for all we know."

Sadness weighed her down as she fought against despair. Not knowing anything about her family made her feel very much alone. "I don't think I am."

Angelica hopped up and down. "I know. We can call you Angel, but that is kind of my name. So, maybe we could call you Christmas or Mary— yeah, Mary, like the mother of Jesus."

They all laughed. "I would have some big shoes to fill. Why don't we go with Miss, or if that doesn't seem right, how about Chris, short for Christmas?"

Angelica clapped her hands. "Yes, Miss Chris it is!"

Mark put his hand on Angelica's shoulder. "We're going to bring the car around to the entrance. I'll leave you in good hands."

She watched Mark and his little girl leave. Geneva followed her look. "Do they remind you of someone?" Her tone was gentle.

"I don't know—maybe. He is so kind."

"Yes, he is. His wife, my daughter, Lily, passed away a couple of years ago, and he has struggled with his grief. Christmas is still hard for us both without her. We have Angelica to celebrate for, but I have to admit, having a guest this Christmas is a welcome thought."

"I don't mean to be rude, but I hope someone will discover I'm missing before then. Or my memory will come back, once I'm away from the hospital."

"Of course." Geneva laid the canvas bag on the bed.

The patient peeked and saw a pair of black leggings and a long red sweater. She lifted her gaze to Geneva. "Thank you."

"Does it look like something you would wear?"

She took another peek. "It looks warm, and I've been so cold."

Geneva pressed her lips into a satisfied smile. "I've brought new underwear for you, too. I imagine they have your clothes you came in with, so they'll have your bra." She pushed the call button.

Moments later, a nurse came into the room. "Are you ready to go, Miss Chris?"

"How did you—" Her cheeks heated, and she laughed. "Angelica, right?"

"Yes. She stopped by the nurses' station to tell us she named you. We thought it was pretty cute. She gave a long spiel about how you couldn't be called Mary, like the mother of Jesus, because you couldn't fit into her shoes. It was quite entertaining."

The patient met Geneva's eyes, which were filled with amusement. "I do hope you are used to little girls," Geneva said.

"I somehow think I am."

Geneva waited outside the room while the nurse helped the patient into her new clothes. When the wheelchair was brought in, she carefully settled into it.

The nurse handed her a plastic bag with the clothes she had been brought in with. "These will need to be washed. They got dirty and wet from your fall."

An orderly pushed the wheelchair to the elevator. Geneva walked beside them. "Our house is about a half an hour from the hospital. I hope you won't be too uncomfortable riding that far."

Panic rose at the thought of riding in a car. For some reason, she didn't like car rides. Her breathing became shallow as the orderly parked her wheelchair beside an SUV. Mark stood there with the passenger door open, waiting. The orderly took her uninjured elbow and helped her stand. She started to walk toward the car, but a wave of panic swept over her. She found herself unable to move. "I can't—I can't ride in the car."

Mark's eyebrows shot up, disappearing into the wave of hair over his forehead. "It's the only way to our house. We live in the suburbs."

She chewed the inside of her lip. "I can't—I don't ride in cars."

"You had a nightmare about an accident. Maybe you were in an accident before you moved to Chicago?" he suggested.

How could she possibly know that? She sensed his frustration, but anxiety didn't ease. "Is there a bus or a train we can take?"

"There is a bus that goes from here to our neighborhood. But it will take an hour and it will be crowded. It wouldn't be good for you with your concussion. You need to get somewhere and rest."

"Oh." She bit her lip and brushed away her tears. "I can do this. I don't know why I'm so afraid."

Mark helped her into the passenger seat of the SUV and shut the door. Geneva sat behind her with Angelica in her booster seat. She gripped the seat so tightly, her hands were turning white. Had she ever had panic attacks before?

"I'm so excited that you're coming home with us, Miss Chris!" Angelica beamed, her eyes shining. "I can't wait to show you my room and my toys and my bed—"

"She's coming to our house to rest, Ange." Mark's scolding was gentle. He glanced sideways at his passenger, and they shared a smile.

"She'll see the Christmas lights on the outside of the house. And our lighted-up Nativity set."

"That sounds very nice." She rested her head against the seat cushion. Her ribs were starting to hurt from sitting upright. She laid her hand across her middle.

"You can tilt the seat back," Mark said. "There's a lever on the side."

She gripped the lever, then tilted the seat far enough that the pressure wasn't on her ribs. She sighed with relief.

"Is that better?" The concern in Mark's eyes was genuine. He was such a caring man, and it was easy to see he was a good father. And a faithful son-in-law. She wasn't sure about the circumstances—why he and his daughter lived with his late wife's mother—but it appeared they had a strong relationship. He must miss his wife very much.

Angelica's chatter continued as they drove through the city. They arrived in a neighborhood with large old trees and brick homes. He parked in the driveway of a ranch-style house with Christmas lights dripping from the eaves. Sure enough, there was a Nativity setting on the snow-covered lawn.

"Oh, Nana! We forgot to turn the light on for the Nativity. It's so pretty when it's lighted up, Miss Chris." Angelica unbuckled her seat belt, opened the door, and took off toward the front steps. Her cast didn't seem to slow her down. She stood with her hand on her hip, tapping her foot. "Hurry up, Daddy. Let me in the house so I can show Miss Chris the manger with Mary and Joseph and baby Jesus!"

"I'll unlock the door and let her in," Mark said. "Geneva, wait for me. It might be slippery out there."

"Oh, I'll be fine," Geneva said, but she stayed seated. So did the passenger.

Mark took his keys out of his coat pocket and unlocked the door. Angelica turned the handle and pushed it open, then disappeared into the house. In seconds, the manger scene lit up.

Angelica ran back to the car and flung open the passenger door. "Do you like it, Miss Chris?"

"It's beautiful, Angelica." The scene brought tears to her eyes. It was as if the lights and the holy family were welcoming her home. She had a strong sense that her life had included faith.

Mark walked back to the car, passing her door. "I'll help Geneva in, then come back for you," he said over his shoulder.

She watched as Mark took Geneva's elbow and walked slowly with her, supporting her, as they went up the cement pathway to the front steps. She realized why Mark was so concerned when she saw that Geneva wore high-heeled red pumps instead of boots. She remembered then that Geneva's coat had been open when she arrived at the hospital room, and she was wearing a bright red pantsuit. Her gray hair was set in stylish waves, and she wore lipstick.

Mark's mother-in-law was an attractive woman. She wondered what his wife had looked like. She must have been beautiful if she'd inherited Geneva's genes.

Mark turned as Geneva walked into the house. When he came toward the car, he grinned. Her heart beat a little faster.

He turned serious as she stepped out of the car. "Be careful now; it's slippery. We got some new snow this morning while we were at the hospital."

She took Mark's hand, and he put his other arm around her waist. They stepped away from the car, and he kicked the door shut with his foot. He set a slow pace for them, but the movement increased the pain in her ribs. She gasped as she took the first step up to the porch.

Mark leaned in. "You're in pain, aren't you?"

"My ribs are really hurting." Each step was painful. Once inside the entryway, she gripped the pillar that rose from the half wall to the ceiling, separating the entryway from the large living room, and held herself up.

"We'll get you to the sofa, and you can rest and take a pain pill."

He helped her take off her coat and hung it up. Then, he knelt and unzipped her boots and took them off while she balanced against the pillar.

It wasn't an open floor plan, but she could see to the right of the entryway that there was a large eat-in kitchen. When she saw the kitchen, her stomach growled.

Mark straightened and looked at her.

"I'm so hungry."

"Didn't they bring you breakfast?"

"They brought it right after you left this morning the first time. I tried to eat it, but I fell asleep before I could finish it. You remember that when I woke up, I was having a nightmare. So, I never ate anything after that."

"You should have mentioned it. I would have brought you something from the cafeteria."

She made a face. "Hospital food? I'd rather have good old biscuits and gravy."

Mark chuckled.

Geneva smiled at her. "You must be from the South."

"How could you tell? Because I like biscuits and gravy?" It was a southern thing, wasn't it? How did she know?

"You have a distinct accent. It's quite adorable."

Geneva's comment made her face heat. She glanced at Mark. He was grinning. Did he think her drawl was adorable, also? She brushed her hand over her hair. She hadn't taken time to shower at the hospital. Her hair was limp and probably had dirt in it from where she'd fallen in the street. The mirror at the hospital had revealed a face that was pale beneath the abrasions. She guessed that Mark was seeing her at her worst. She didn't want to think too long about why it mattered what he thought of her.

"I really could use a shower."

Mark squeezed her shoulder and guided her into the living room. "First things first. Let's get you settled and fed. You can take your pain medication while you're eating."

Angelica grabbed her hand. "I want Miss Chris to come see my bedroom and my dollhouse!"

"Not right now, Ange." Mark's tone was patient. "She got hurt, remember? She needs to eat and then take some pain medicine. And rest." He stressed the last word, and Angelica pouted.

"I got hurt, too. And my arm hurts right now."

"Then we need to get you some pain medicine, and you can rest on the sofa with Miss Chris." He winked at the guest.

She let Mark lead her to the long tweed sofa with plump cushions. After she was settled on one end of it, he moved a footstool in front of her. She sat back and sighed. "Much better than the hospital bed."

He grinned.

Geneva stood at the end of the sofa, her hands folded in front of her. "Scrambled eggs and toast would be easy on your stomach, to go along with the pain pills."

"I like my eggs over easy, if it wouldn't be a problem."

Geneva's eyes widened.

Mark's eyebrows shot up.

Her comment was as much of a surprise to her as it was to them. "My memory seems to be coming back in flashes."

"They assured us at the hospital it was temporary," Mark said.

"It was *likely* temporary."

Angelica tapped the guest's forehead. "We have to think positive thoughts. That's what my mommy used to say." Her voice trailed off.

There was strain on Mark's face at the mention of his wife. It appeared that his grief was still very real, even though his mother-in-law told her Lily had died two years ago.

The guest patted Angelica's cheek. "Your mommy was right. We have to have a little faith."

"Do you believe in God, Miss Chris?" Angelica's eyes were wide with hope.

"I don't know. I believe in God; surely, I do."

Angelica danced in place. "Will you come to my Christmas Eve program?"

The guest looked at Mark to see whether he would extend the invitation. He grimaced. "I don't think she'll feel like going to church tomorrow night. Like I said, she needs to rest."

Geneva brought in a plate with two eggs and crisp, lightly browned toast.

Her stomach growled, and she reached for the plate.

"Just because you won't go doesn't mean she won't want to." Geneva frowned at Mark. "Now, what would you prefer to drink, Miss Chris? Something hot—coffee or tea, perhaps? Or iced tea, milk, or juice?"

"Tea sounds great. Is it sweet?"

Mark's eyes were warm when he grinned at her. "That's another southern thing." Geneva turned toward the kitchen, but Mark touched her shoulder. "I'll get her tea and her pain pills."

After Mark left the room, Angelica sat down beside the guest and leaned in close. "Daddy doesn't go to church anymore," she said in a voice that was too quiet for the energetic little girl. "He doesn't believe in God because God let my mommy and the baby die."

The guest's eyes filled with tears. "Oh, I think I understand his feelings," she whispered.

Geneva sat in her recliner opposite the couch. "Maybe you lost a loved one in a car accident, and that's the reason you're having flashbacks and don't like to ride in cars?"

"Maybe." She thought of the nightmare she'd had. Mark had told her there had been no blood when she was hit by the car. Had she been in a car accident before yesterday? She had no memory of it, but maybe subconsciously, she remembered.

Mark walked back into the room. He held out the glass of tea and a couple of pain pills. Since she couldn't get a prescription without her identification, the hospital had sent home a few samples. She took the pills and swallowed them, then drank some of the tea. The tea tasted bitter, and she wrinkled her nose. She ate a couple of bites of egg and bit into a piece of toast.

Angelica looked up at Mark and patted the other side of the sofa. He sat down and crossed his ankle over his knee.

The guest looked at them and at Geneva. They all belonged together. It wouldn't take much for her to feel a part of this family. She sighed and took a sip of her tea. "I wish I could find out where I belong."

"You belong with us, doesn't she, Daddy?" Angelica swung her gaze from the guest to Mark.

"She's my Christmas wish come true."

His brow furrowed. "What exactly did you wish for, Ange?"

"I wished for a new mommy so you could be happy again."

His face flamed. He rubbed the back of his neck, and his mouth formed an angry line. He looked around as if searching for an escape route. He wouldn't meet the guest's eyes.

It was clear he wasn't looking for a new wife, even if Angelica had wished for a new mother. For some reason, the fact that he wasn't ready for a new relationship made the guest sad.

She put her arm around Angelica's shoulders. "It's lovely that you wished for your daddy's happiness. But I'm sure he still misses your mommy very much and doesn't want someone to replace her."

"Not yet, anyway," Geneva put in softly.

Angelica turned to Mark and buried her face against his chest. She sobbed. "I'm sorry, Daddy. I want a new mommy so bad."

His anger faded into a look of tenderness. He brushed his hand over Angelica's hair and kissed her forehead. "I know you miss your mommy. But it has to be someone special, that I choose, not someone you wish for. And our guest is right. I'm not ready for a new wife yet. I don't want to replace your mommy with someone new."

Geneva tsked.

The sound brought anger back into Mark's eyes. He glared at Geneva. "I suppose you put her up to this."

"Do you think I'm ready for another woman to take my daughter's place?" To the guest's ears, her protest was mild. It seemed Geneva hoped her son-in-law would marry again.

She finished eating and set the tray on the coffee table. Her movement brought them all back to reality.

Mark gave her an apologetic look. "We're making our guest uncomfortable with this talk."

He was right, but she didn't say it aloud.

Angelica's sobs had subsided. She pushed away from Mark's chest. "Feel better now, Ange?" he asked.

She sniffled. "I guess so. I'm hungry."

Geneva stood and held out her hand to Angelica. "Let's go make some sandwiches, sweetie."

Angelica put her hand in Geneva's, and they left the room.

Mark turned to the guest. "What can I do for you?"

Her body was aching. The pain pills hadn't started to work yet. "I think I'd like to sleep a little while."

"We don't have a guest room, but I'll change

the sheets in my room, and you can sleep in there. I'll sleep on the sofa tonight."

Her face flamed. The thought of sleeping in Mark's room felt too intimate. "No, I don't want to put you out of your room. The sofa is fine, for now, anyway. And who knows? Maybe by tonight, there will be news on my identity."

CHAPTER NINE

THE THOUGHT OF SOMEONE COMING TO claim his guest stuck with Mark as he went to the linen closet to get the extra pillows that were stored there. Angelica's wish had thrown him for a loop. She missed having a mom in her life so much that she was wishing for a new one.

He gripped the edge of the closet door as a wave of emotion overtook him. He'd lost a wife and a child. Angelica had lost her mother. Lily had made their daughter her whole world. He'd thought Geneva had been a good replacement for Lily, loving Angelica as she did, but his daughter was old enough to have memories of her mom. To remember what it felt like to have a mommy to tuck her in at night, to sing silly songs with her, all the things Lily had done so well.

Even a new wife for him could not completely

replace Lily in his daughter's life.

Why did his thoughts immediately go to his guest when he thought of marrying again? As stunned as he was at Angelica's revelation of her wish, his guest had responded to Angelica's outburst with gentleness and kindness, giving his daughter the answers that he couldn't come up with.

He brought the pillows to the living room. "Are you sure you'll be okay on the sofa?"

At her nod, he plumped the pillows and put them on the edge of the sofa. He waited while she shifted and lay back, holding her injured arm in its sling across her chest.

"Would you like a blanket?" She nodded. He took the afghan from the back of Geneva's recliner and covered her with it. "How is that?"

The smile she gave him warmed his heart. "Okay, then. Sleep well." Mark walked into the kitchen, where Angelica and Geneva sat at the table. They were almost finished with their sandwiches.

Geneva had left the sandwich fixings on the counter. He fixed a turkey-and-cheese sub. He added sliced tomatoes and lettuce, then mustard and mayo.

"How is our guest?" Geneva asked when Mark sat down.

"It won't take her long to fall asleep, I don't

think. The pain pills are pretty powerful." He ate a couple of bites of his sub. "I worry she'll have another nightmare."

Angelica raised her curious gaze to him. "What kind of nightmare?"

Geneva shook her head slightly. Mark cleared his throat. "It was nothing. What are the two of you going to do this afternoon?"

"I have a little more shopping to do," Geneva said.

He grimaced. "Shopping two days before Christmas? Don't you know that's going to be a nightmare?"

"Is that the kind of nightmare Miss Chris had? A shopping one?"

Mark bit his cheek as he tried not to laugh. Geneva's shoulders shook, although she kept from smiling.

"I don't think so. What are you shopping for?"

Geneva shrugged. "Some last-minute gifts."

So, she wasn't going to be forthcoming with any more information. "Must be a secret."

Angelica giggled. "We can't tell you, Daddy."

"Since you're going shopping, I think you might want to pick up a couple of gifts for our guest, in case she's still here on Christmas morning."

Angelica clapped her hands. "Yes, we need to buy her something!"

Geneva's eyebrows rose. "That's a nice gesture."

Mark ignored the question in her eyes. They had already discussed that he was getting involved with their guest. He wasn't going to confirm it. "I know I was hesitant to bring her here, but I'm glad we did. She's safer here than she would be on her own, even in a women's shelter."

Angelica was focused on his words. He reached over and ruffled her hair to avoid a question he didn't want to answer.

"What should we buy for Miss Chris?"

Mark was grateful Geneva was redirecting the conversation. "Maybe some perfume?" That had been one of his go-to gifts for Lily.

Angelica nodded. "And a book?" She rested her chin on her hands. "What kind of books does she read?"

"I don't know," Mark said. With amnesia, she probably wouldn't know what books she liked to read, either, or whether she enjoyed reading.

Geneva folded her arms on the table. "We can get her a new purse, since someone stole hers. I'm not sure what her style is, but I think we can find something."

"That's a good idea!" Angelica's head bobbed. "I want to pick out a purse."

Mark could imagine a purse with unicorns and hearts on it. "Maybe you should let Nana buy the purse."

Angelica pouted. "What can I buy for her, then?"

Geneva patted her hand. "I'll help you find something special."

Angelica jumped up, ready to leave. "Are you going shopping with us, Daddy?"

"No, I don't want to leave our guest alone. I'll stay here in case she needs something." Mark ignored the knowing look from Geneva. He took out his debit card. "Why don't you take this with you and purchase the gifts with it?"

She didn't take it. "I can pay for them."

"If you like." Neither of them mentioned that Geneva was on a fixed income. The money she thought would see her through retirement had been depleted by her husband's bad investments. Mark paid the household expenses, and Geneva took care of Angelica. She refused to take a salary for that. Their living arrangement was a win-win for all three of them.

Of course, that might change if he decided to marry again. Although he couldn't imagine marrying someone who wouldn't love Geneva and want her to be part of the family. It would have to be someone pretty special. His mind wandered to their unexpected guest.

After Angelica and Geneva left for shopping, Mark went into his room to change the sheets.

When he and Lily moved in, Geneva insisted on giving them the master bedroom. Lily hadn't wanted to sleep in her parents' room, so she'd decorated it in a Hollywood glam style, with lots of gold and white, to make it hers and Mark's.

After Lily passed away, he couldn't stand to stay in the room; it held so many memories of her. Geneva had suggested he redecorate, and she'd helped him choose rich, masculine colors. It had been cathartic to paint over the white walls and change the carpet. It looked like a new room. He hadn't been able to sleep on the mattress he'd shared with Lily, though. Her scent lingered, making his grief worse. He'd purchased the mattress and box spring after he repainted. Even though he wiped out every trace of Lily from his bedroom, he couldn't escape the memories.

He stripped the sheets off the bed and put on a set of floral ones that he'd never used. It felt strange to think a woman would be sleeping in his bed tonight. There had been only one woman in his life. He'd vowed after Lily died that he was never going to get married again.

He sighed. Angelica wanted a new mother. And although Geneva said she wasn't ready for someone to take Lily's place, she sometimes tried to set him up. Mark chose not to date anyone. He didn't want to. In fact, he hadn't found any woman even remotely interesting until yesterday, when he'd met the woman who saved his daughter.

Angelica and Geneva thought she was sent here by God for Mark. Even his assistant had that idea in her head.

He couldn't think about starting anything with this stranger, even though the tender feelings he felt for her were starting to take root. She might be married or engaged, ring or no ring. And she was sweet right now, but who was to say their personalities wouldn't clash when they got acquainted, after she got her memory back?

If she got her memory back.

Mark walked into the living room and paused by the sofa. The guest slept with her uninjured arm over her head. Her hair had fallen back, showing the lump that was evidence of her heroic act. Abrasions covered her left cheek, but they didn't appear to be deep. They would probably heal without leaving scars.

With her sleeping and Angelica gone, the house was quiet. Mark took his laptop to the kitchen table and checked his email. He'd received one from the opposing counsel in the Denton divorce case. He opened the attachment and read the amended offer of settlement.

With a satisfied smile, he leaned back. His client would not have to go out and get a job after all. The husband had agreed to pay the amount of alimony they'd asked for.

Family law had not been on the horizon when he left law school. He'd taken a job as an associate in a firm that defended insurance companies. He'd been good at what he did and made partner earlier than he hoped.

But after Lily passed away, Mark's work as a trial lawyer took a beating. He couldn't function at work. His partners had suggested he take a three-month FMLA leave to cope with his grief. During those twelve weeks, he'd taken up running, even though it'd been winter. The time he spent in the fresh air—and the exercise that made him sweat—had helped clear the fog of grief from his mind.

He'd spent a lot of time at home, too, holding Angelica and playing games with her. In the beginning, she had cried so much, not understanding why her mommy was no longer with her. Cuddling with his daughter while she cried had helped Mark release his tears.

By the end of the twelve weeks, he'd been ready to go back to work. He hadn't wanted to go back to the seventy-hour weeks, focusing on billable hours. Instead, he ditched the high-powered firm and took over Lily's family law practice. He inherited her client base and, in the past two years, had increased his business to the point that he was thinking about hiring an associate.

Right now was not the time for that. First, he

had to go through the process of getting used to a new assistant. The thought of working with someone new made him nervous, but Shannon had insisted her replacement would be a good fit.

Mark dialed the number for his client. She must have been out shopping, by the noise of the crowd and Christmas carols in the background. "Merry Christmas, Mrs. Denton," he said after introducing himself.

"Does your call mean my husband settled?" Her voice was giddy.

Mark grinned. He always enjoyed a client's reaction to good news. "Yes, he agreed to the amount we were asking for."

"Oh, thank you, Mr. Harper." Her words caught on a sob. "I can't thank you enough."

"Do you have time tomorrow to meet and sign the paperwork?"

"Of course, I do." She said it as if he'd asked a silly question.

Maybe he had. "I'll have Shannon set something up and call you with the time."

After hanging up with his client, Mark called Shannon at the office. "How's everything going without me?" he asked tongue in cheek. They often joked that she could do his job for him.

"Just fine, Boss. What's going on with you?"

"I have a guest for Christmas. Well, for as long as she needs a place to stay, anyway." He kept his voice casual.

Shannon was silent.

Mark laughed. He'd made his chatterbox of an assistant speechless. "I brought home the woman who rescued Angelica. It was Geneva's suggestion, but it made sense. The hospital was going to release her, and we didn't want her to end up in a women's shelter with her amnesia."

"I'm just—I'm just amazed that you would bring a strange woman into your home. You haven't wanted anything to do with another woman since Lily died."

Her implication made him defensive. "She'll stay until the amnesia wears off or until relatives come for her. I'm not planning to marry her." A little doubt niggled at him, but he brushed it off.

"I didn't think so, but wow!" She cleared her throat. "So, what are you going to do to help her find her family?"

Mark rose and moved to the doorway between the kitchen and the living room. He leaned against the doorframe as he focused on his guest. "The news station wanted to put a picture of her on the air and social media and share that she has amnesia. I talked her out of doing that."

"Why would you do that?"

He moved back into the kitchen. If Shannon doubted him, maybe he should have done things differently. "Anyone could have shown up at the hospital and said he was her husband. If she couldn't remember him, she wouldn't know the truth. It was for her safety."

"I get that. You might want to rethink that decision, though. She's safe now with you. And you could work with the police to do a background check into anyone who claims a relationship to her, you know."

Shannon's reasoning was almost always on point. That's what made her so valuable in his practice. He could bounce ideas off her, and she would give him honest feedback. It was going to take some time to develop that kind of relationship with a new assistant.

"You're right."

Shannon laughed. "I'm always right, Boss. You know that."

He chuckled. "Yeah, right. So, how do we do this—get a picture to the news station? Would they have to come out here and talk with her again?"

"No, just check with her and make sure she's on board with it. If she is, snap a picture on your phone and text it to me. I'll pass it on to the right people at the news station, and they can take it from there. We should say that anyone who responds should contact the police if they know her."

He sat down. "Good thinking. The police have my number, so they can get ahold of me."

After a couple of further instructions, Mark ended the call with Shannon. He closed his laptop and carried it back to the entryway. As he stashed it in its leather case, he looked over the half wall into the living room. The guest had awakened and was starting to sit up. He zipped up the case and walked around the corner.

As he moved toward the sofa, she looked at him with a startled expression. "I'd forgotten where I was for a moment."

He sat in the recliner across from her. "No nightmares this time?"

She shook her head, then winced. She reached behind her and rubbed her neck, rolling her head around. He thought about asking whether she wanted him to massage her neck but thought better of it.

"So, I might have misled you yesterday," he said.

Her eyes widened.

"When I told you that it wasn't a good idea to share your photo on the news report and social media, I might have made the wrong decision."

"No, you were right. Anyone could have seen that picture and contacted the hospital. I felt safer not doing that."

"Well, I'm glad you felt that way. I think you may want to go in the other direction today. Now that you're safe here with me..." His voice trailed off as her gaze met his. Her deep brown eyes showed trust and a hint of attraction. He broke eye contact with her and looked at a spot over her injured shoulder. "Now that you are in our home, you have a safe place to meet any person who says they know you. If they're not familiar to you, we can take their name and information to the police, and they can investigate that person to make sure they are who they say."

"So, we should let them post my picture on the news?"

"And ask anyone who knows you to contact the police."

She smiled. "That should stop any crazies from coming around."

He swung his gaze back to her and saw the amusement at their shared joke. He grinned.

She stood. "If you're going to take a picture of me, I'm going to shower first." He started to protest. She waved a hand over her face. "I can't do anything about the cuts and bruises, but my hair is gritty from the dirty pavement."

"If you want to shower, then let me get you some towels and show you where everything is."

"Does your mother-in-law have a T-shirt I can borrow, instead of putting this sweater back on? The nurse helped me dress at the hospital. It was pretty painful with the broken collarbone, and if I'm going to shower, this sweater isn't going to go back on easily."

His gaze landed on the forest-green tunic sweater that hugged her feminine curves. He quickly lifted his head and refocused on her eyes. "I don't know what Geneva has in her closet, but I'll get you a T-shirt of mine. It will go over your arm easier."

Mark went to the linen closet and took out a couple of fluffy towels. Then, he went into his bedroom and took a plain blue T-shirt out of his drawer. He paused for a moment, picturing her wearing it. Then, he shook his head to erase the image. He brought both the shirt and the towels to her.

"Here you go. Geneva has some bottles of shampoo and soap. You can use whatever you need."

Her cheeks were pink, and he realized she felt as uncomfortable with this as he did.

"So, I'll leave you to it." Mark walked into the kitchen. He paused a moment as he heard the bathroom door click shut. "She's a vulnerable stranger," he reminded himself out loud as he prepared a pot of coffee. "Get your mind back where it belongs."

CHAPTER TEN

SHE STOOD IN THE STREAM OF the shower, holding her arm with the broken collarbone close to her ribs. There was shampoo and conditioner on the shelf. She hoped her hair would be manageable. It had a few snarls from lying in the hospital bed. She washed and rinsed her hair, but it was awkward with one arm. Then, she studied the bruises on her arm and rib cage.

All she could remember about her life was that she had woken up in a hospital bed—and everything that had happened since.

In a way, it was like beginning over. She had no idea where she'd come from or what she had left behind. Was it so wrong to want this to be her life now? Mark was so kind and so handsome. She could see that he was attracted to her, as she was to him. She also knew he didn't want to be. He wasn't done grieving the loss of his wife. Somehow, that made her sympathetic toward him. It seemed as if she had known a great loss herself.

Angelica was a sweetheart. So full of energy and joy. She was glad that she had stepped in and saved her from getting hit by the car. Even hurt as she was and with amnesia, she knew she would do the same thing again. Angelica's life was valuable. Mark loved his little girl very much. It had clearly torn his heart when she admitted she had wished for a new mommy. It was one thing he couldn't— or didn't want to—give her. He'd admitted that he was not looking for someone to replace his wife.

That made her a little sad. She could get used to being a part of this family. Even though Geneva was the mother of his late wife, she had a good relationship with Mark, as though he were her son. She didn't know why they all lived together, but it seemed to be working for them.

The water started to cool. She turned it off and stepped carefully out of the tub. Pain shot through her ribs, and she leaned against the wall. When she could catch her breath, she toweled off. It was a struggle to get dressed. She pulled on the leggings she'd been wearing before the shower and then eased into the T-shirt Mark had given her. It was several sizes too big and hung to her knees, but it covered her modestly. As she moved toward the mirror above the sink, she caught the masculine scent from the bottles of aftershave and cologne on the counter.

It felt intimate, being in Mark's home. In the bathroom where he washed and shaved. Wearing his T-shirt. He'd been so kind to her, so gentle and tender as he helped her into the house and took off her coat and boots. It was easy to see that he was a good man. She would be foolish to take any of his actions personally, though. He was being kind to her because she'd saved his daughter—perhaps not from death but from serious injuries.

She walked into the living room, where Mark stood waiting for her. His gaze swept over her in the too-large T-shirt and leggings, lingering for a moment. He cleared his throat and held up his phone. "Shannon wants a picture of you, remember?"

She wrinkled her nose as she held out her arms. "In this shirt?"

"We only need a photo of your face. Shannon can crop the T-shirt out."

"All right. Let's do it." She stood straight and still while he snapped a couple of pictures.

He held his phone up and showed them to her.

"Oh, yuck." She grimaced as she saw the pale face with the skinned-up cheek. "Do I really look that bad?"

"Not to me, you don't." He flashed a grin. Was he flirting with her?

He focused on his phone while he texted the photo to Shannon. "She'll take care of it from here."

The smell of pizza came from the kitchen. Her stomach rumbled.

Angelica walked into the living room. She stopped and stared. "Why are you wearing my daddy's T-shirt?"

"It's big, so it was easy to get on with my arm being hurt."

"It took you a long time to get ready. Now, we can finally eat."

Mark frowned at Angelica. "That was rude, Ange."

Angelica ducked her head. The guest patted her on the shoulder. "It took extra time to get dressed using only one arm. Did you bring pizza?"

Angelica's head bobbed. "It's the best pizza in Chicago." She spun around and half-walked, half-danced toward the kitchen.

The guest watched her go, an image of another little girl coming to mind. It was blurred, and she couldn't make out the features. Though she tried to focus, she couldn't bring up a memory to go along with the image. Was there a child in her life? How horrible to think she might have a family that she couldn't remember. She hoped when the TV station showed her picture on the news tonight, someone would call and identify her.

Mark picked up the sling she'd left on the coffee table. "I think you're going to want to wear this." He held out the sling, helped her slip her arm into it, and lifted the strap over her head. Her hair flowed beneath it.

She reached up at the same time he did to lift her hair out from under the strap, and their hands touched. He was so close she could see the hints of gold in his brown eyes. He had a trim beard, giving his strong jaw a rugged look. She licked her dry lips, and his attention fixed on her mouth. Heat rose into her cheeks.

He completed the process of lifting her hair out from under the strap, then stepped back. "How's your pain level?" He asked the question like he was a doctor, cool and impersonal. Hadn't he felt anything when they were within kissing distance?

She got a grip on her emotions. "I could use some pain medication with my pizza."

"We'll get that for you." He rested his hand at the small of her back and guided her toward the kitchen.

Two large pizza boxes sat on the table. "It smells really good," she said, sitting down in the chair Mark held out for her. "Is it deep dish?"

"How do you know?" Angelica asked.

"Well, you said I'm in Chicago, and I guess…" Confusion filled her, and she glanced at Mark. "I don't know how I know some things and not others."

Angelica put her hands on her hips in a diva pose. "Are you sure you really lost your memory, Miss Chris? You don't seem to have nam-neesha."

She laughed, and Mark did, too. "I really wish I knew my name, sweetie." The laughter was replaced by sadness. She couldn't help the emotions that choked her.

Angelica wrapped her arms around her waist and hugged her. The feel of the little girl's body pressed against her hip was a familiar one. A blurry face flitted in and out of her vision, and she tried to bring it into focus so she could remember. Maybe she had a child of her own somewhere? Why did that make her sad and not happy? Maybe something bad had happened—the nightmares…

Angelica leaned back and looked at her. "You're nice. I wish—"

Mark pulled out Angelica's chair. "Sit down, Ange, so we can eat." He opened the box nearest him.

It looked good, with sausage and pepperoni and some other kind of meat. There was pepperoni and mushrooms on the pizza in the other box.

"Which one do you prefer?" Mark asked.

She hesitated. She had no preference one way or the other. She shrugged. "I guess pizza is pizza. I'll eat any of it."

"My favorite is the one with the pepperoni and mushrooms," Angelica said with a hopeful expression.

"Then, I'll try that one first." She took a slice and put it on her plate.

Mark's eyebrows drew together. "Hopefully, you're not allergic to mushrooms."

She smiled. "I guess we will find out, won't we?"

There was silence as she took a bite of her pizza. A strand of cheese clung to her slice. She broke it off with her fingers and stuck it in her mouth along with the pizza. She chewed and swallowed. "Oh, this is really good." She looked around, and three smiling faces looked back at her. "I don't think I've ever tried this before."

"If you had, you would probably remember," Angelica said in a matter-of-fact way. "Since you really like it."

After finishing her first piece, the guest chose the one with the three meats for her second helping. She was about to say she liked it more than the first, but when she saw Angelica's eyes on her, she couldn't hurt the child's feelings. She winked at her. "They're both really good, but I like the flavor of the mushrooms on the first piece."

"Are you going to help us decorate Christmas cookies tomorrow, Daddy?"

Angelica's question surprised her. Mark was

an attorney. It was hard to imagine him baking. Did he wear an apron? She pictured him in a frilly one and coughed to cover a laugh.

"If you wait until I get home. I'm going to the office in the morning."

Geneva frowned. "On Christmas Eve?"

"I've managed to settle the Denton divorce case."

Geneva's forehead pinched. "Is my friend going to have to get a job?"

"No. Her husband settled on what we were asking for. She'll manage to keep up her lifestyle without interruption."

"She should be able to. He's the one that left her for a woman half her age." Geneva huffed. "After forty years of marriage, he should have to keep supporting her."

The legal talk felt familiar to the guest.

"I'll close the office at noon so I can help you decorate the cookies." Mark's gaze slid to hers.

"So, you decorate cookies?" she asked.

"Yes. For the past two years, I've helped."

Since his wife passed away. She thought she understood—he'd stepped in to fill the empty space in the holiday tradition. "So, this is a family thing?"

"Yes, it is, but you're welcome to join us," Geneva said with a smile.

"If you're still here." Mark sounded almost as

if he hoped she would be gone. The contentment she felt this afternoon burst. When her gaze met his, he looked apologetic. He must have realized his words hurt. "For your sake, I hope you remember who you are. It's a tough time of year not to be with family."

"And someone is probably worried about you." Angelica looked at her grandmother. "Isn't that what you said, Nana?"

"Yes, that's why we can't promise you she'll be here for Christmas. Because she belongs to somebody else."

"That makes me sound like a lost kitten."

"A brown-eyed kitten," Mark said. His face turned red as the women stared at him.

So, he had noticed that their guest had brown eyes. Who wouldn't notice? They were her best feature, dark, with thick lashes. They glowed in the lights above the table. Mark realized he was staring.

She smiled, apparently amused at his expense.

"Well, I think I've had enough pizza." Mark drained his glass of milk. So what if he was a grown man and still liked to drink milk? Especially with pizza. Combining soda with spicy sausage and sauce gave him heartburn. The milk washed the pizza down and soothed instead of burned.

How old was their guest? Did she even know? Probably not, as she couldn't remember the other details about herself. Geneva cleared her throat. He looked around and saw that Angelica was watching him, expecting him to answer something he hadn't heard. "What were you saying, Ange?"

"That if no one else claims her, like a lost kitten, then we get to keep her."

It was a good thing the milk had gone down already, because it would have sprayed out of his nose. He covered his face with his hand, keeping his head bowed so Angelica wouldn't realize how hard he was laughing. It was an innocent statement but wrong on so many levels. He dared to glance at their guest. She, too, was trying to cover her laughter.

Geneva gave them both a stern glance. "That isn't the way it works with people, Ange."

"Well, I didn't know that!" Angelica scowled at Mark, then at their guest.

Mark got his laughter under control and, with a straight face, reached out and took Angelica's hand. "Well, now, you know, Ange. But I have confidence that her family and friends are looking for her."

He knew he sounded like he was trying to get rid of her. Maybe he was. This attraction he felt to a perfect stranger was something that he was fighting against. He didn't intend to get into a relationship with any woman or marry again. As far as he was concerned, he'd had a perfect wife, and no one could take her place. But that didn't keep his gaze from wandering over her long dark hair and taking in the deep brown eyes with the long, thick lashes.

She blushed, and he realized he was staring again. He directed his gaze back to Angelica. "Is it time to watch our Christmas movie now?"

"Yes, tonight, it's about the mean man who steals all the presents." Angelica turned to the guest. "It's the really old cartoon one that Daddy watched when he was a kid."

"Daddy's not that old," Mark said, trying to keep a sheepish grin off his face.

"How old are you?" Her dark eyes held interest.

"I'm thirty-three."

"If you had to guess my age, what would you say it would be?"

Geneva tsked. "A lady never asks a gentleman to guess her age."

"And a gentleman would never attempt to guess." Mark smiled at the warmth in her eyes.

"I would guess that you are around thirty," Geneva said. They looked at her. "What? It's okay if another lady guesses."

Their guest stiffened, and she reached for her broken collarbone.

Mark saw it and the grimace on her face. "Time for pain meds." He got them off the counter and handed them to her. She swallowed them with her glass of tea.

"Are you going to watch the movie with us, Miss Chris?" Angelica asked.

Despite the plea in Angelica's big brown eyes, she shook her head. "No, sweetie. I'm going to go to bed." Her cheeks were flushed as she looked at Mark. "Are you certain you want me to take your room?"

He grew a little uncomfortable at the thought of her sleeping in his bed, but he nodded. "Yes. You need a good night's sleep. I know you didn't sleep well on the sofa earlier."

He held out his hand, and she put hers in it. He tugged her to her feet, but instead of letting go of her hand, he held it for a few moments. Another tug, and she would be close enough to kiss. At the moment, he wanted nothing more, but now was not a good time. And when she figured out who she was, it might never be the right time for them.

He squeezed her hand. "I'm glad you are here, Miss Chris," he said in a husky tone.

Her eyes filled with sadness. She tugged her hand free and walked out of the kitchen.

He'd been honest when he said he hoped, for

her sake, that someone would identify her. She deserved to be with her family, whoever they were. Selfishly, he wanted her to stay a little longer. He didn't like his growing attraction to her. He hadn't been looking for a relationship, but the attraction seemed to be mutual. He wondered how she would feel about him when she had her memory back. Would she go back to her home and forget about him, or would they be able to stay in touch?

CHAPTER ELEVEN

THE GUEST WALKED DOWN THE HALL to Mark's bedroom, her heart heavy with grief. She knew he'd wanted to kiss her. She'd wanted him to, until he called her "Miss Chris." He didn't know who she really was, because she didn't know, either. Until she regained her memory, there couldn't be anything between them.

She walked into the master bedroom and looked around. The room was decorated in masculine colors. The walls were a deep blue, and the carpet was the color of coffee. There were maroon accents throughout, including the bedspread. Had Mark changed it after his wife passed away? Even with the new sheets—which she knew he'd put on just for her, as they were flowered—his clean, manly scent lingered on the pillow. The mattress was so comfortable, but it was hard to relax.

She'd left the door open. Mark had insisted, in case she needed something in the night.

Even though she'd declined to watch the movie, she could picture the scenes. She must have seen it many times, perhaps as a child. Why were some things familiar and other things—the important things—a mystery? She was still awake when the movie ended, and she could hear Mark as he tucked Angelica in bed across the hall.

Then, his tall frame filled the doorway. When he saw she was awake, he stepped inside, keeping some distance between them. "How are you feeling?"

"I'm not able to relax yet. I'm afraid I'll wake up with nightmares."

Mark moved the desk chair over beside the bed. In the dim light from the hallway, she could see his features. Dark eyes, warm with compassion, met hers. Her breath caught. How could she have feelings for a man she just met, when she didn't even know her name?

He wrapped his hand around hers. A strong, masculine hand but not rough and calloused.

"You've suffered trauma, and your body is probably still recovering from the shock." He sounded like an authority on the subject. "It's going to take a few days before you're feeling like yourself again."

She giggled.

His eyes narrowed. "What did I say that's so funny?"

"How can I feel like myself when I don't know who I am?" He smiled, and, oh, was he handsome! She wondered whether he could feel her pulse picking up speed. She tried to slow it by keeping things casual. "So, you don't think I'm a Chicago native?"

He rubbed his thumb across her knuckles. Traitorous pulse. From the way his lips twitched, she suspected he knew what he was doing to her. "You weren't raised here, not with that accent. It's hard to tell how long you've been living here."

The cold Chicago wind had chilled her to the bone when she left the hospital. She still felt a little chilled, especially in this T-shirt. "I agree. I feel so cold, so I don't think I'm used to Chicago's winter weather."

"That means you're fairly new to the city. I wonder why you came." He removed his hand from hers, and the warmth fled with it. He tapped his chin. "Let's play a guessing game."

"Okay. Maybe I came to visit relatives for Christmas."

He nodded, smiling slightly. "Which means they're looking for you. That's a good thing. Or maybe you came for work. I should check with the hotels in town and see if there are any conventions taking place."

"I doubt it, this close to the holiday. But maybe I did come for a job."

"Your coat and boots aren't practical for Chicago weather. If you came for a job, you haven't been here long. Maybe you came to get married." Mark studied her hand.

She followed his gaze to her ring finger. There was a faint line, as though she had worn a ring at one time. "I don't think I came here to get married. Or that I am currently married or engaged. But I was, at one time."

Mark traced the faint line around her finger. Then, he looked at his own. "It looks a lot like mine. You must have lost someone a couple of years ago."

"Maybe I'm divorced. It would explain the move to Chicago."

He moved his hand to her forehead and smoothed her hair back. "Maybe you're a widow. You were having nightmares about a car crash, a child screaming, blood—"

Tears filled her eyes.

"Are you remembering?"

"No, but if I am, that would have been a sad way to lose a husband and child." His touch was soothing. "How did your wife die?"

"She was seven months pregnant and went into early labor. There were complications—"

She touched his hand. He didn't flinch away.

"She was in so much pain," he said in a raw voice. "And she was so afraid. So was I. I didn't want to lose her."

She heard footsteps on the carpet outside the room. Geneva stood in the doorway, illuminated by the light from the hallway. "How are you, my dear?"

Mark stood, and the mask was back in place. It was a shame that he hid his pain from those who loved him.

"I think I'll be able to sleep now." Her eyelids felt heavy, but she didn't want Mark to leave. He was so kind and tender with her.

"Good night, then." Geneva walked away.

Mark moved the chair back to the desk and stood in the doorway. "Good night."

"Good night. Thank you for talking with me. It helped."

He nodded and left the room. Not long afterward, she fell asleep.

CHAPTER TWELVE

MARK TRIED TO GET COMFORTABLE ON the sofa. It was long enough to stretch out on. He'd purchased it for that reason. It wasn't the length of the sofa that was making him uncomfortable, though.

Memories of Lily were warring with the attraction he felt to his guest. She didn't resemble Lily, but she was like Lily in that she was sophisticated and very feminine. She was taller than Lily—the top of her head reached his chin. He'd noticed when he was releasing her hair from under the sling. He had been so close he could hear her breathe. He hadn't been that close to a woman since Lily passed away. He'd had to fight against the temptation to move those few inches and kiss her.

He'd felt it again in the kitchen. That time, it hadn't scared him as much, but he'd had to corral his desire because she was in a vulnerable position in his house.

And then, he had sat with her in his room, holding her hand. He knew that his touch affected her. It had made him want to find a deeper connection, to find out more about her and discover who she was. She seemed to fit so naturally into his home.

He tried to remind himself that he wasn't interested in finding a wife.

Yet, even though he wasn't looking, this woman had appeared in his life in a dramatic way. There had to be a reason. He didn't believe what Angelica did—and apparently Geneva, also—that God brought this woman into his life to become his wife. He didn't need one. His life was full. He worked long hours, but his priority was always Angelica. He took her to the aquarium and museums, often accompanied by Geneva. In the summer, they visited the Navy Pier and walked around downtown. Life was so unpredictable, and he wanted to fill Angelica with good memories.

He was a good father, but that didn't fill the empty spot that Lily's death had created. That spot was the shape of Lily, and he'd been unwilling to see it any differently. Now, this wonderful, beautiful woman had come into his life, into his home, and reminded him how lonely he was. Her smile, her laugh, the warmth of her dark eyes—she was creating her own place in his heart.

With thoughts of the past and present blending, he tossed and turned. He was still looking at the clock at 1 a.m. but drifted off to sleep. A scream pierced the quiet house, and Mark jolted awake, heart racing. He jumped up and ran down the hallway to the bedroom where their guest was sleeping. She was sitting up in bed. He sat on the bed and wrapped his arms around her, holding her against his chest until she calmed.

"I'm sorry," she whispered, pulling back. "I don't know why I have these nightmares."

"Is it the car crash again?"

"Yes. I just keep hearing the child screaming, and…"

He patted her back. "Don't let yourself think about it anymore. Angelica is fine. You're okay. You're safe here."

Geneva appeared in the doorway with Angelica.

The guest covered her mouth with her hand. "Oh, I'm so sorry. I didn't mean to wake everyone."

Angelica ran over to the bed and hopped up beside her. Then, she put her arms around the guest. "I'm sorry I ran out in front of the car and scared you."

She squeezed Angelica's shoulders. "I don't think that's what scared me, sweetie," she said in a gentle voice. "I think something bad happened before I met you. A car accident where someone close to me died. I don't remember it. But it's still in my mind because I see flashes of it. That's what causes the nightmares."

"Don't be scared." Angelica smiled wide. "I know—let's pray for you!"

"Oh, I don't—"

"Don't turn down a child's offer to pray." Geneva's admonishment was gentle. "It's a season for miracles."

Angelica prayed a sweet, simple prayer that the bad dreams and nam-neesha would go away. The adults had to bite their lips to keep from smiling at her mispronunciation. When she said "Amen," their guest hugged her. "Thank you. I believe God heard your prayers."

"I know He did, because He loves us."

Mark gritted his teeth. He didn't agree with Angelica. He'd wrestled with his doubt for the past couple of years. Meeting Geneva's eyes, he saw her frown. He knew better than to argue with his daughter. Geneva would kill him if his lack of faith rubbed off on Angelica.

"Back to bed, Ange."

Angelica flopped against the pillow. "I don't

want to go back to bed."

Mark picked her up, and she tried to escape his arms. "Angelica." At his stern tone, she stopped struggling. He brushed her hair back from her forehead. The lump was still visible. She'd had a rough couple of days, and she was overly tired. His voice gentled. "You need to try."

"How about I make some hot cocoa," Geneva suggested. "We can all have some, and maybe it will help us get sleepy again."

Geneva led the way out of the room. Mark waited for their guest to follow, then carried Angelica out.

As they walked along the hallway, their guest said, "I'm so sorry for waking everyone up."

"Don't worry about it. You've been through a terrible trauma," Geneva said.

As they entered the living room, the guest asked, "Do you want some help with the cocoa?"

Geneva shook her head. "No, it only needs one person to stir it."

Mark set Angelica down. He scooped up the bedding he'd been using on the sofa and set it at one end. He made a sweeping motion as their guest looked at him. "We might as well get comfortable. It will be a few minutes before the cocoa is ready."

Angelica plopped onto the sofa. She tugged at Mark's and their guest's hands until one was seated on either side of her.

Before Geneva had the cocoa ready, Angelica fell asleep. Seeing his daughter nestled against the beautiful stranger filled Mark with a sense of rightness. He drew in an unsteady breath. Was he falling for someone he didn't know, who didn't know herself?

"I'll carry her to bed." He stood, gathered Angelica into his arms, and carried her down the hall.

Geneva brought two steaming mugs of cocoa into the room. She handed one to the guest. "Where are Mark and Angelica?"

"Angelica fell asleep, and Mark carried her to bed."

Geneva smiled and shook her head. "That child. I didn't think she'd be able to stay awake long. How are you, my dear?"

The guest blew on the hot liquid, then took a sip. "I'm feeling better. I don't know why I keep having nightmares."

"I'm sure everything is all jumbled together in your mind right now."

"That's a good way of putting it."

"You've been good for him, you know."

Geneva held her gaze.

"I don't think he's looking for a relationship. He's been very clear about that." He'd drawn a line in the sand when Angelica expressed her Christmas wish. Although, when he was holding her hand earlier, that line had been a little blurry.

"Sometimes, God allows circumstances to change our way of thinking."

Mark came into the room. Geneva rolled her eyes and inclined her head toward him, smiling around her mug.

He glanced from one woman to the other. "What did I miss?"

"You didn't miss anything," Geneva said.

He didn't look convinced, but he let it go. He nodded toward the mug in Geneva's hand. "Do you have a cup of cocoa for me?"

She tapped her chin. "Well, let's see. I brought two into the room with me. One for our guest and one for Angelica. Since Angelica fell asleep, I'm drinking hers." Geneva smiled. "I guess yours is still in the pan."

"I see how it is," he said. "You offer to make cocoa, and I have to get it myself." He grinned as he spun away toward the kitchen.

"How long have you and Mark lived together?" She still found their living arrangement a little odd.

"Lily and Mark moved in with me when my

husband died. I had some financial difficulties, and they helped pay expenses. After Lily passed away, Mark asked if I wanted him to move out. I told him it was his choice, if he wanted to find a place of his own. We both agreed that we needed to keep life as normal as he could for Angelica, so he stayed. He's never talked about moving out again."

"Will you be okay if he—moves on from Lily?"

"You may find it hard to believe, but I want Mark to be happy again, even if it means marrying again. I hope he'll choose someone who won't mind a former mother-in-law in their lives. If she does, well, then, it will be time for me to move out."

Mark walked into the room, frowning at Geneva. "You're not moving anywhere." She started to argue, and he shook his finger at her. "If the woman I choose for a wife can't love you, then I can't love her. It's as simple as that."

Geneva winked. "Notice that he's thinking about choosing a wife now?"

He scowled. "I am not." With the blankets piled at one end of the sofa, he didn't have a choice but to sit in the middle. He wasn't any closer to her than he'd been earlier, but Angelica wasn't sitting between them. Warmth radiated from his body, and she caught the scent of his cologne. His scowl relaxed into a grin. "Geneva, you pulled that one out of me on purpose."

The guest shared a smile with Geneva, then curled her legs under her. Pure contentment filled her as she sipped her cocoa, until she remembered why she was here.

Geneva finished her cocoa and set the mug on the coffee table. "I'll let you take care of that, Mark. I'm going to see if I can catch a few more hours of sleep."

She watched Geneva leave. "Your mother-in-law is a wonderful person."

"I know. She likes you, too."

"Is it important to you that she likes me?" For some reason, it was important to her to know that.

He grimaced. "I would say that I value her opinion, but she has tried to set me up with nearly all the single daughters of her friends. I don't think she has very good judgment."

"Why not?"

"Because she wasn't the one who set us up and you're the first woman who has caught my eye since—in a long time."

Heat filled her cheeks at his admission. He took her empty cup from her and set it on the table with his. Her heart rate picked up as he moved closer and put his arm around her shoulders.

"I don't know why I'm doing this," Mark whispered before pressing his lips against hers. The joy she felt fulfilled a longing that she hadn't known existed, a desire to belong somewhere. She wanted to belong to this man, this family, even though she was unsure whether she already had a family of her own.

He broke off the kiss and moved back. "I'm sorry. You're very vulnerable right now, and I shouldn't be taking advantage of you."

"You're not taking advantage of me," she said softly. "You're not that kind of man."

His eyebrows lifted. "How do you know?"

"You are too kind and good."

He stroked her cheek. "I have a feeling you are, too."

She leaned into his palm, savoring his touch. "Maybe I'm really a horrible person. I don't know."

His gaze held hers, as if he were searching her soul. "You aren't. I wouldn't be attracted to you if I thought you were a horrible person."

"I think I'll be able to sleep now. The cocoa helped, and you..." She lowered her gaze at the intensity in his eyes and stood. "Good night, Mark."

He stood and faced her. He laid his hands on her shoulders. "You mean 'Good morning.'" He gave her an irresistible grin. When she smiled, he leaned down and kissed her forehead. "I hope you sleep well."

She gave a little wave over her shoulder as she

walked down the hallway toward the bedroom.

CHAPTER THIRTEEN

MARK WOKE AT SEVEN O'CLOCK, AN HOUR later than his usual time. He'd slept on the sofa because there was a beautiful woman in his bed. A beautiful stranger that he'd kissed last night. He had no business kissing her when she was suffering from amnesia. There were too many things about her that were unknown. Most importantly, was she free to love him? Because he was falling for her in a big way.

He didn't feel rushed to get ready for work. Shannon had set the time for his meeting with Mrs. Denton at ten o'clock. He didn't have anything else on the calendar for today. He was supposed to stay home and help Geneva and Angelica bake cookies. It had been Lily's tradition to bake cookies with her mother for the reception after the Christmas Eve program.

When Geneva got the ingredients out last Christmas Eve and told Angelica it was time to bake cookies, Angelica had started to cry for her mommy. Geneva had tried to comfort her, but she ended up breaking down, too. Mark had walked into the kitchen and gathered them both into his arms. Then, he helped bake and decorate six dozen sugar cookies.

He got up from the couch and folded the blanket, then set it neatly at the end and plopped the pillow on top of it. He wondered how long he was going to have to sleep on the couch. Not that he minded, given the circumstances, but he was feeling a crick in his neck this morning from the awkward sleeping position. He put both hands on the back of his neck and stretched it.

He didn't really want to get ready and go to the office. He enjoyed cutting out the sugar cookies—and especially decorating them. Last year, he and Angelica had started a contest to see whose cookie was decorated the best. Since Geneva couldn't remain impartial—or so she said—he'd sent photos to Shannon for her to judge them. Of course, she picked Angelica's, which Mark had made a big deal about. It was about building happy memories with his daughter and carrying on his wife's tradition, with his own twist.

He'd brought out a change of clothes last night so he wouldn't have to go into his bedroom this morning. As he passed his bedroom on the way to the shower, he forced himself not to peek inside. Just the thought of her in his bed stirred his senses. Their guest would be here for the cookie decorating this year. He wondered whether that would change the dynamics. He wanted the focus to be on Angelica, but it would be pretty hard to ignore the beautiful woman who'd taken up space in his heart.

Mark showered and dressed in his suit. He put on the tie Angelica had bought for him when Lily was alive. At the time, he'd been horrified at the thought of wearing it. It was red with green Christmas trees. He'd worn it to the Christmas Eve program that year and received many chuckles and comments on it. Angelica had been so proud of it. Last year, he hadn't gone to the program, so he'd taken it out a couple of days before Christmas and worn it to his office when he didn't have court. He remembered how tickled Angelica had been when she saw him wearing it.

He didn't know what the respectable Mrs. Denton would think of it. Hopefully, she had a good sense of humor, because he didn't want to disappoint his daughter.

He had to pass his bedroom on the way back to the kitchen. This time, he couldn't help himself. He paused in the doorway and looked in. He wanted to know all about the beautiful stranger whose dark hair fanned across his pillow, the stranger he'd found such a strong connection with. How old was she? Who was she?

He'd held a secret wish since their tender moments a couple of hours ago. He wanted her to stay for Christmas. Angelica would be heartbroken if their guest left. He should not have told her and Geneva to buy gifts for her, but Angelica was so excited about giving her presents on Christmas morning, and Mark hadn't been able to tell her no.

In the kitchen, he whipped up an egg-white omelet with peppers and mushrooms Geneva kept prepared for him in the fridge. He made two pieces of whole-grain toast. Lily had started him on a heart-healthy diet in the months before her death. Her father died of heart disease, and Lily wanted Mark to live a long and healthy life. Instead, she had been the one who passed away before her time. He kept to the diet at breakfast and carried the lunch to the office that Geneva insisted on packing for him, same as Lily had. He tried to tell his mother-in-law she didn't have to do it, but honestly, he was thankful at midday to have a sandwich and apple to eat when his often-busy schedule made taking a lunch break difficult.

Geneva walked into the room. She poured a cup of coffee for herself and sat across from him. "How is our guest?"

"She's sleeping yet." A picture of her asleep against his pillow came into his mind, stirring tenderness in him. "I feel so bad for her with these nightmares she has."

"They are terrible flashbacks, aren't they?" Her lips pressed together. It meant she was about to say something serious. Mark held his breath. "Mark, Angelica didn't want me to tell you—"

At those words, his heart dropped.

"Tonight, she's singing with the children's choir."

He let out the breath he'd been holding, relieved it wasn't something bad. "Really? I thought she was too young to sing in the choir."

Geneva shrugged. "They included kindergarteners this year."

"Ange is the only one in her class, isn't she?"

They attended an old traditional church, and most young families were choosing contemporary churches. There weren't many children, and Angelica was currently the youngest. Not that it made a big difference for him, as he hadn't attended since Lily's death.

"She is. I think that's why they included her. They didn't want her to feel left out of the program."

Mark gave a frustrated shake of his head. "Why didn't she tell me?"

Geneva patted his hand. "She knows you

don't want to come. She didn't want you to feel like you had to go."

He knew his daughter well. "That doesn't sound like her. She would normally make sure I do something she's involved in."

"I think she's worried she might make a mistake in front of you."

"Now, that sounds like Ange." Mark stood, rinsed his plate and mug, and set them in the dishwasher. Another change he and Lily had made when they remodeled the kitchen. Geneva hadn't wanted one at first but agreed that it made her life much easier.

There was no traffic when Mark drove into the city. He parked in the garage and was surprised to see Shannon's car in her parking space. He walked into the office to the smell of fresh coffee and the light, flowery perfume that was Shannon's scent.

She was in the break room. Unlike her usual business-casual attire, she wore leggings and a tunic sweater with high leather boots.

"Going casual today, I see," Mark said. She gave him the usual light hug. Her familiarity had bothered him at first. She treated him as she had Lily—as a friend as well as a boss. Ten years older than Mark and happily married for twenty years, she was more like an older sister than an employee.

"How is your guest? Any news yet on her identity?"

"No." What would Shannon say if she knew he had kissed her in the middle of the night and couldn't wait to do it again? "What are you doing in the office? I thought you took today off."

Shannon shrugged. "I came in to get papers ready for Mrs. Denton to sign."

"You know I could have printed the documents myself, right?" He was computer literate and knew how to create and edit documents. "But I appreciate you coming in and doing it."

She grinned. "Only so many more days to make your life easy, Boss. Then, you're on your own."

"I thought you found me a great assistant."

Her grin widened. "I did. I think you'll be happy with my replacement."

His mind switched to his guest. "Did the TV station run her photo last night?"

"And this morning. They posted it on social media, too."

"That's good. I hope someone contacts the police about her soon." Mark tried to hide his disappointment at the thought of her leaving, but

Shannon was observant.

"You don't seem in a hurry to find out who she is. Is there something I should know about?"

At her knowing look, heat rose in his face. "It's Christmas. She should be with her family."

"Uh-huh." Shannon grinned. "Keep telling yourself that."

Shannon prepared the documents. Mark met with his client. Mrs. Denton sobbed as she signed the divorce settlement. She capped the pen, stood, and sighed. "Thank you so much, Mark. I'm so glad it's over."

He put his arm around her shoulders as he guided her out of the conference room. "You're welcome. I'm glad it worked out so well for you."

After Mrs. Denton left, Mark handed Shannon the signed document. She emailed it to the opposing attorney, who was meeting with the husband this morning. Within a half hour, the attorney emailed it back, signed by both him and the husband.

"After Christmas, I'll call the court and get a hearing date," Shannon said.

Mark checked his watch—eleven thirty. "I think it's time to close up the office and go celebrate Christmas."

They rode the elevator to the main floor and walked to the parking ramp together. Shannon held out her arms for a hug.

Mark hugged her, thankful for her help and sad that she would soon be leaving him. "Merry Christmas, Shannon."

"Merry Christmas, Mark. May all your wishes come true."

He thought of Angelica's wish for a new mommy. He'd been so angry when she told him that. He'd been convinced he wasn't looking for a new wife. Somehow, though, by last night, he'd been thinking it might not be such a bad idea after all. He needed to find out his guest's identity for an important reason. He could see how well she fit into his family, and being with her filled the emptiness in his heart.

He grinned as he backed out of the parking space. Maybe Angelica's wish was rubbing off on him.

CHAPTER FOURTEEN

THE GUEST WOKE TO THE SMELL of something sweet baking and the sound of a child's laughter. Looking at the clock on the bedside table, she was shocked to see it was ten o'clock. It was later than she was used to sleeping. She gave a little self-conscious laugh. At least, she didn't think she slept this late. It was frustrating how some things she could remember but the important ones still evaded her.

She walked to the kitchen in her pajamas. Angelica knelt on a chair, flour on her cheek, trying to roll out dough with one arm. Geneva stood next to her, wearing a Christmas apron, ready to help. They looked up when they heard her. Their smiles were welcoming.

"You're finally up!"

She tried not to laugh at Angelica's rude

comment. "I slept really late, didn't I?"

"Prob'ly 'cause you have nam-neesha and forgot what time you got up."

That was the most illogical and cute explanation. She sat down to watch the pair work. She brushed away a few crumbs of cookie dough and rested her arms on the table. "It was probably because I woke everyone up in the middle of the night. None of us got a full night's sleep. I'm sorry."

Her gaze went from Angelica to Geneva. The older woman smiled. "No need to be sorry. Your body is recovering, and your mind is trying to as well. I'm sure the flashbacks are normal after what you've been through."

Geneva's kind words brought tears to her eyes.

"Can I fix you an omelet?" Geneva asked.

"Oh, that does sound good. I'll get dressed first." She jumped up from the chair.

"I left a T-shirt of mine on the sofa for you, if you want to wear it while we bake," Geneva said. "It might fit over your sling all right."

The guest looked down at Mark's T-shirt that she had worn to bed. "It might fit better overall."

"Go ahead and get changed. I'll have breakfast ready for you when you're done."

On her way through the living room, she picked up the red T-shirt from the sofa. She held it up in front of her, grinning at the elves decorating a Christmas tree. She didn't think it was something she would pick out for herself, but it was cute and appropriate for a casual Christmas Eve. Plus, Geneva was a couple of sizes larger than her, so hopefully she'd be able to get her injured arm into the sleeve without too much painful pulling.

After a bit of a struggle to get into the T-shirt, she carried her sling to the kitchen. A hot omelet and a steaming cup of coffee waited on the table for her. "Thank you, Geneva. You're spoiling me."

Geneva smiled. "You look like you need a little spoiling." She came around the table and reached for the sling. "Let me help you with that."

With her sling in place, she sat down and picked up her fork. She ate a few bites of the omelet. "This is very good, but I think I usually eat biscuits and gravy for breakfast. It's what comes to mind."

"I'll bake some biscuits for tomorrow morning. I make a pretty good sausage gravy, not as good as what you are used to, I'm sure, but I think you'll enjoy it."

"If I'm still here."

"Why wouldn't you be here, Miss Chris?" Angelica's dark eyes were round.

She didn't want to disappoint Angelica. "Maybe today, someone will find out where I am and claim me. Then, I'll spend Christmas with my family, whoever they might be."

Angelica's eyes welled with tears. "You're my Christmas angel. You have to spend Christmas with us."

Geneva smoothed Angelica's curls. "She has a family who is missing her. We've talked about this."

"I'm going to sing in the children's choir tonight. Will you come to my program?"

For some reason, she didn't think she wanted to be in church, but she couldn't stand the thought of breaking the little girl's heart. What would it hurt, even if she was discovered by family today, to spend an hour in church and watch Angelica sing?

"I would like to see you sing, but I can't promise I'll come. I hope you understand."

"I guess. Having nam-neesha is no fun."

"No, it isn't." She ate her omelet, watching Angelica use old tin cookie cutters to cut out the shapes. Her grandmother put them on a baking sheet, and soon, the smell of cookies baking filled the kitchen.

CHAPTER FIFTEEN

A TABLETOP COVERED WITH BAKED SUGAR cookies greeted Mark when he walked into the kitchen, but the sight and sounds of the three females melted his heart. Angelica wore her child-sized apron, she had flour on her cheek, and her hair was up in a high ponytail. His mother-in-law—a standard figure in his life for the past ten years—wore her Christmas apron, her hair in a bun.

He had to admit, though, that neither of them set his heart racing like the sight of their unknown guest. She wore a white apron with a ruffle, and her hair was pulled up in a high ponytail like Angelica's. He wondered whether she had done his daughter's hair or whether Geneva had tried something new. Undoubtedly, it was their guest. She had flour on her cheek, also, and he wanted nothing more than to wipe it away with his thumb and feel the soft skin underneath.

They all looked at him, three smiles of greeting. He couldn't help but grin. "Looks like I'm in time to help decorate the cookies."

"Wash your hands first," Angelica said in her little bossy manner.

"Of course." There wasn't a lot of space to get

past their guest, and their shoulders brushed. He stifled the urge to put his arm around her waist and stand close. He could smell the light scent of shampoo. Thankfully, it was not the kind of shampoo Lily used. Geneva had listened to his request to wipe that trace of Lily from his life and switched shampoos and soaps to a scent that didn't remind him of Lily.

He washed his hands, and soon, he was absorbed in icing and decorating reindeer, Christmas trees, bells, and snowmen.

"Are you coming to my Christmas program, Daddy?"

Mark exchanged a look with Geneva, glad for her intervention earlier to let him know how much Angelica wanted him there. "Yes, I'm coming. I wouldn't want to miss watching my Christmas angel sing."

She giggled. "Miss Chris is going to come, too."

"Is that right?" Mark looked at their guest with interest.

"Yes. If no one comes for me before then, I'll go to the program. I want to hear Angelica sing, and Geneva said it's a candlelight service. I think it sounds very peaceful."

Geneva's eyes glowed. "It is peaceful. When we sing 'Silent Night' and light our candles at the end, it brings us to the true meaning of Christmas."

Angelica put her hands on her hips and studied their guest. "Do you know the true meaning of Christmas, Miss Chris? Or can't you remember it?"

The guest smiled. "I think I remember it, but why don't you tell me, anyway? In case I've forgotten something."

Mark listened to his daughter tell the story of the Nativity. As she talked about Joseph and Mary and the birth of baby Jesus, he realized it was Lily's version. He glanced at Geneva. She smiled at him.

"And God sent Jesus to earth to be our Savior, to save us from our sins. Jesus was God's gift to us, and that's why we give gifts to those people we love at Christmastime." Angelica finished her story on a proud note. She looked at their guest.

"How very lovely, Angelica."

"Nana taught it to me. She said my mommy believed it."

A knot formed in Mark's chest. Lily believed in the miracle of Christmas and the gift of salvation every day of her life. In fact, he wasn't raised in a home where God was talked about. There had been so much anger in his childhood home. Lily had taught him to love God. It was because of her that the story of Christmas meant something to him.

"You had a very smart mommy." She laid her hand on Angelica's shoulder and touched her

147

cheek to the top of Angelica's ponytail, as though savoring the little girl's scent.

Mark wondered again whether she had a child and husband who died in a car accident. What if she never learned about her previous life? Could he go forward with a woman who didn't know her past? When they finished icing and decorating six dozen sugar cookies, they all helped clean the kitchen. Geneva prepared shrimp cocktail for a light supper before the Christmas Eve service. After they ate, it was time for Angelica to take her bath.

Mark and their guest sat on the sofa while Geneva took care of Angelica's bath. "How are you doing?"

"I'm okay." She didn't sound okay.

"Do you miss your family?"

"How can I miss what I don't know?"

"That's true." He moved close enough to cover her hand with his. "I'm sorry you haven't heard from any of your family or friends yet."

"I don't understand the why of it. I know things happen for a reason—at least, that's what people say. But what good can come of not knowing who I am or where I belong?"

"Maybe you'll find a new identity and a new place to belong." As he said the words, he wanted them to be true. He had known her only two days, but she was already ingrained in his heart.

Angelica came flying out of the bathroom, dressed in a red velvet dress with a ruffled skirt and white rose buttons on the bodice. It was tied with a white sash. The red of her cast almost matched the color of the dress. Her wet hair hung down her back. "Would you like me to braid your hair, Angelica?" their guest asked.

"Can you braid?"

"I think I know how to braid a little girl's hair. Do you have some ribbons we can weave into it?"

"I know where they are." Angelica hurried down the hallway to her bedroom. She came back with red ribbons, the ones Lily used to put in Angelica's braids.

Geneva had tears in her eyes. "I have arthritis in my hands. I haven't been able to braid Angelica's hair. I can barely brush it."

Mark couldn't watch the stranger comb Angelica's hair as his daughter knelt on the floor in front of her. It was too heartbreaking to think of Lily sitting there, doing that same thing many times over. He was glad when his cell phone rang, giving him an excuse to leave the room.

He walked into the kitchen and answered the call, surprised to hear from Shannon on Christmas Eve. "Is everything all right?"

"How is your guest doing?" Shannon asked.

"She's okay, I think. She's going to the Christmas Eve service with us."

"That's wonderful. I have a confession to make, Mark."

His heart stopped for a second. "What kind of confession?"

CHAPTER SIXTEEN

A S THE GUEST'S FINGERS NIMBLY BRAIDED Angelica's hair and wove the ribbons in, she realized she had done this same act many times before. Her emotions choked her as she tried not to break down at the overwhelming memories.

Serena Cole.

That's who she was. She was from North Carolina. This was her first winter in Chicago. Her first week, actually. She'd left her hometown behind to start a new job.

Her daughter, Maggie, would have been the same age as Angelica.

Maggie—

The devastating loss of her husband and daughter came back to her in waves of grief. It wasn't the incident with Angelica that gave Serena nightmares, although it likely had triggered them.

The nightmares were from the accident that had taken the lives of Tom and Maggie eighteen months ago. She'd come to Chicago to start a new job. She knew no one in the city. There would be no family or friends looking for her.

Her hands shook, but she finished Angelica's braid. It was Angelica's special night. She needed to keep her emotions under control for the next hour and a half so she didn't upset the little girl who had come to mean so much to her.

That meant hiding her secret, the fact that her amnesia had worn off, until after the Christmas Eve service.

She tied off the ends of Angelica's braids. "You are all set, sweetie."

Angelica stood and hugged her. "Thank you, Miss Chris. Now I'll look beautiful for my program."

Serena gently moved past Angelica and started down the hallway. She managed to get all the way into the bedroom before breaking down. She shut the door and leaned against it. Her whole body shook. She thought she'd worked through her grief over Tom's and Maggie's deaths. She'd also lost her mother in November. She'd made the decision to take the job in Chicago, hoping to leave her painful memories behind.

With the amnesia, she'd forgotten everything about her past. She'd started to form a bond with

Mark and his family. All her memories were now coming back to her, and so was the grief.

A knock sounded on the door. "It's almost time to leave," Mark said. "Are you ready?"

She looked down at the Christmas T-shirt splattered with flour and icing. Her hair must be a mess. "Almost," she said through the door.

She waited until she heard him walking away before she opened the door and slipped into the bathroom. She stripped off the T-shirt and pulled her familiar green sweater over her head. When she looked in the mirror, it wasn't a stranger who looked back at her this time. Her eyes were puffy from crying, and there was flour on her cheek. She splashed some cold water on her face and dried it with a towel. Then, she took out her ponytail holder and brushed her hair.

Her eyes started to well with tears again. She shook her finger at the reflection in the mirror. "You can do this. You only need to keep it together for a little more than an hour. Remember, it's Angelica's night." She opened the bathroom door and walked into Mark.

He put his hands on her shoulders and looked down at her. She averted her gaze, hoping he wouldn't see that she'd been crying.

"Are you all right?"

She pasted on a smile and held up her sling. "If you can help me with this, I'll be ready to go."

He didn't dawdle over helping her put the sling on. She was glad. If he had taken her into his arms right then, she would have started weeping. Somehow, she knew, in Mark's arms, the pain and grief she'd felt for the past months would melt away.

There was no time to tell Mark she had her memory back. She would wait until after the program ended, then ask him to take her to her hotel.

Geneva and Angelica were waiting in the living room. Serena put her hand on Angelica's shoulder. "Are you ready, Angelica?"

Angelica's head bobbed. "Are you ready, Miss Chris?"

She gave a genuine smile then. She'd come to like the nickname that Angelica had given her. How would Angelica—and Mark—respond when she told them she knew her real name and her story? The confession would have to come later. "Yes, I'm ready to hear you sing."

This time, she had no fear of getting into the SUV. Geneva insisted she sit in front. When Mark drove up to the church door, he got out and helped Angelica out, then opened the door for Serena.

He took her hand and supported her as she stepped onto the salted pavement. "Be careful. It might be slippery."

Angelica put her hand in Serena's as they

walked up the church steps. "Can I tell you a secret?" she whispered, coming to a stop outside the door.

So, Angelica had a secret, too? "Of course, you can, sweetie."

"I'm scared about singing."

Serena took the little girl's hands in hers. "Are you scared about getting up in front of everyone?"

Angelica nodded. "I know the words, but I'm afraid I won't remember them."

"How about if you look at me when you're singing, and I will mouth the words if you forget them?" Serena knew the Christmas carols Angelica and the children's choir were going to sing. It was a medley of familiar old songs.

"Okay, I'll do that." Angelica squeezed her hands and then disappeared downstairs, where the children were gathering.

Mark appeared beside Serena and helped her off with her coat, then hung it up. Then, he took off his and hung it next to hers. As they started up the stairs to the sanctuary, it seemed every man and woman there wanted to talk to him. He introduced Serena as their guest. Some of them knew the story of Angelica's rescue, and her cheeks burned when they praised her for her heroic actions. She had a hard time holding her tongue when they questioned her about her amnesia. Mark was helpful in sidestepping that question.

They followed Geneva to the third pew from the front. It was too close to the front for Serena's comfort, but she wanted to help Angelica. Even though she was pretty sure the child would remember all the words, because she was so bright, she wanted to be easily seen.

Although all the children were beautiful and festively dressed, Angelica seemed to stand out. Standing in the front row, three children from the microphone, she sang with all her heart.

"Why does she stare at you when I'm right here beside you?" Mark whispered.

"She was afraid she would forget the words. I told her to watch me and, if she forgot, I would mouth them to her."

"She hasn't missed a beat."

"I know. She's wonderful, Mark."

He took her hand, entwining their fingers. She smiled at him. When she looked back at Angelica, there was a bright smile on the girl's face. What was that all about?

When the program was over, Angelica came back to sit with them and wiggled into the seat between them, forcing their hands apart. She took their hands and brought them back together across her knees. She sighed.

"You did wonderfully," Serena whispered.

"I didn't forget any of the words," Angelica whispered back. Or tried to whisper, anyway. She put both her hands on top of Serena's. The warmth of Mark's hand in hers and Angelica's hands on top sealed the longing Serena had developed for this family.

When it was time to light the candles, Angelica begged to hold one.

"I'll help you hold mine," Mark said.

The choir sang "Silent Night" as the flame was passed around the room. When Geneva lit Serena's candle, she smiled at her, a smile that seemed to welcome her home. Serena turned, holding her palm close to the flame so it wouldn't go out.

Angelica held the candle with both hands, and Mark's strong hands covered hers, holding it steady as Serena held her flame to it and lit the wick. Mark's eyes met hers, and the peace she felt as he held her gaze went deep. He turned and lit the candle behind him, then turned back around and helped Angelica hold their candle. When the service ended, he let Angelica blow it out.

As the crowd started to gather their things to leave the sanctuary, Mark turned to Angelica. "Ready to go home, Ange?"

"No! I want to stay for cookies!" The peace of the candlelight service was broken.

"We're not staying tonight."

Angelica kicked the back of the pew in front of them. "But I want to stay. I helped decorate the cookies for it and everything."

Mark took her hand and pulled her to her feet, gentle but firm. "Your bedtime will be too late if we stay. You want to get a good night's sleep tonight."

"Yes, because you'll probably be up early." Serena recalled the last Christmas with Maggie when she was old enough to understand there would be presents in the morning. Maggie had woken her and Tom at 5 a.m. so she could open gifts. "I knew a little girl who couldn't wait to get up on Christmas morning to see if there were presents under the tree."

Over Angelica's head, her gaze met Mark's. Instead of looking confused, he smiled. She didn't know how, but somehow, he knew who she was.

As they turned to leave, Mark leaned in and whispered in her ear, "It's good to meet you, Serena."

A thrill went through her at hearing him say her name when for two days he had been unable to refer to her as anything other than Miss. Some of the sorrow she'd felt earlier at remembering the loss of her family melted away at the tender light in his eyes. He knew her name. How much more did he know about her? And how had he found out?

CHAPTER SEVENTEEN

A NGELICA'S CHATTER ON THE WAY HOME went over Mark's head as he tried to make sense of the last few hours. Shannon's phone call had thrown him for a loop. She confessed that she figured out who Serena was the evening before, when he'd texted a photo to her. How was it possible that such a coincidence had occurred?

But it had. Or, according to Shannon, it wasn't really coincidence at all.

He glanced at Serena. Her gaze met his, and she gave a shy smile. He'd called her Serena in the church. She'd been surprised that he knew, but he had realized then that her amnesia had worn off. At what point had that happened? And what would she do now?

She was likely staying in a hotel somewhere. Would she ask him to take her back there tonight?

If she left now, it would break Angelica's heart. She was so sure that Serena was her Christmas angel—and the answer to her wish. Geneva had also expressed that Serena had been brought into their lives to save Angelica from serious injury and maybe even for something more.

It was that something more that made his thoughts linger on her. He stole another glance at her. He'd felt responsible for her condition since it was his daughter she had risked her life for. Somewhere along the way, that had grown into attraction, which had blossomed into a tenderness he'd not felt since Lily.

He reached over and found her hand, the one attached to her injured shoulder. She curled hers into his, and he entwined their fingers. In the glow from the streetlights, he could make out the blush rising in her cheeks. If she wasn't free to love him, then she wouldn't allow him the privilege of holding her hand, would she?

He looked at her and squeezed her hand. She met his gaze and smiled. Whatever pain had been in her past, he saw the peace that was evident in her now. That same peace had wrapped around him as he'd held the candle with Angelica. The grief had washed away, and his heart had filled with joy and love. After he put Angelica to bed, he would talk to Serena and learn more about her past. If she was indeed single, would she want to make a new beginning with him?

"Daddy, you haven't been listening."

Mark's face flushed with heat. "I'm sorry, Ange. What were you saying?"

"Did you hear me singing?"

That, he could answer honestly. Although three children away from the microphone, his daughter's pure voice rang out clearly. "Yes, I did. And you sang very well."

"I know."

That was his Ange, self-confident like her mother. The memory of Lily brought a smile instead of the usual pang of sorrow. Was it possible that God had used Serena to bring joy to his life again? Because ever since he met her in the hospital and looked into her deep brown eyes, his heart had begun to lift out of the grief it'd been wrapped in. Being with her made him feel alive again.

As he turned into his driveway, he reluctantly released her hand. "We're home," he said, looking at her. He hoped she could read the truth in his eyes, that he felt like she belonged with him and his daughter. She seemed to really like Geneva as well. If she was going to be a part of his life, then that was a test she'd have to pass. He planned to treat Geneva as a member of his family no matter who he settled down with.

He chuckled as he got out of the car and opened Angelica's door. Wasn't it just yesterday when Angelica had revealed her Christmas wish to him? And he'd told her he wasn't looking for a replacement for Lily? Well, he hadn't been looking, and no one could ever take the place of his first wife, but his heart had expanded and created a new space for Serena.

He made sure Geneva and Angelica made it into the house safely. Then, he returned and assisted Serena as she stepped out of the car. He boldly wrapped his arm around her waist as they walked up to the house.

She stopped on the doorstep and faced him, her hand on his arm. "Mark, my amnesia wore off earlier tonight. And somehow, you've figured out who I am."

"Yes, I found out earlier tonight, and I promise I'll explain everything."

Angelica appeared in the open doorway. "Daddy, Miss Chris, come in the house. Grandma said I have a present to open tonight." She disappeared back into the house.

Mark studied her. "Are you going to tell her what your real name is?"

"No, I don't think so. Let's save that news for a Christmas morning surprise."

He leaned in and kissed her. "Thank you."

Serena walked into the house ahead of Mark. He helped her take off her boots and coat, then guided her into the living room. Angelica stood near the Christmas tree, her hands clasped in front of her. "See, Daddy? There's a present here for me, and it's not even Christmas morning."

Serena sat on one corner of the sofa. He sat next to her. Not close enough so they were touching, but not so far away that she couldn't sense his presence next to her.

"Go ahead and open the package, Angelica," Geneva said from her recliner.

Angelica didn't need to be told a second time. She ran over to the sofa and hopped up between Serena and Mark. She shook the package. "What do you suppose it is, Miss Chris?"

"Let's see…" Serena tapped her fingers on her chin. "I can't guess. I think you should open it so you can find out."

Angelica was tearing the wrapping paper even as she spoke. "Oh, a book! And it's about the Nativity. Look, Daddy!" Angelica held the picture book under Mark's nose. He lowered it a little, and Serena could see he was studying it. The image on the front was the manger scene with light glowing around baby Jesus.

"That's beautiful, Ange." His voice was husky.

He looked at Geneva. She lifted one shoulder, appearing somewhat defiant. Serena was surprised Geneva had bought the book for Angelica, since Angelica had told her Mark didn't believe in God anymore.

"What else is in the package?" he asked.

Angelica lifted the material and shook it out. A long red flannel nightgown with an old-fashioned lace collar and buttons fell out. Fortunately, it had capped sleeves and not wrist-length. It should easily slide over Angelica's cast.

"That's really pretty. And it matches my cast. Thank you." She looked from Mark to Geneva, a question in her eyes.

"It's from both Daddy and me," Geneva said, daring him to say differently. "Something new to wear to bed tonight and a new book to read together."

Angelica hugged Mark, then ran across the room to hug Geneva. Tears formed in Geneva's eyes, and she smiled at him over Angelica's shoulder.

"Thank you, Geneva," he said.

Angelica hurried back across the room. "Daddy, will you read me the story?"

"Don't you think Nana should?"

Serena glanced at Mark. He didn't seem to be upset with the book choice, although she didn't think he had known what book Geneva picked out.

"I thought Nana would read the story to you."

Angelica pushed the book into his hands. "I want you to do it. Your voice is lower."

Serena listened as Mark's deep voice read the story of how God had sent His Son, Jesus, to earth as a baby to save the world from its sin. Mark's voice caught in places as emotion took over. Before the Christmas Eve service, Serena would have thought Mark didn't want to read the story. But now, his voice was almost reverent.

The words sounded like poetry, coming from Mark's mouth. Serena allowed herself the pleasure of listening to the rhythm of his words, stealing glances at his lips. Those lips had kissed her so sweetly and held a promise of a future together. Had he really overcome his disbelief in the goodness of God and found peace? It had seemed that way when they were in the church, when she lit his candle and looked into his eyes. And as he read the Bible story, it was clear he had believed those words once, and it sounded like he did again.

Serena knew what it was like to lose the peace of God. Her life with Tom had been a challenge. Not because of him, but because of his family, who had despised her. She'd thought once Maggie was born, they would accept her as one of them. Instead, they'd shunned Maggie, too. She'd still been shrouded in grief when her mother was diagnosed with cancer. Helping her mother through the long battle with her illness, then losing her, had wiped out her faith.

Waking up in the hospital, not remembering who she was or how she had ended up there, she'd been frightened. Mark had taken her under his wing. She'd felt safe with him. He'd come to the hospital when she was desperate and held her hand. His words had soothed her last night when she'd been trying to fall asleep. He'd held her when she awakened, frightened by the nightmare. And he'd kissed her, not once but twice.

Mark may have let his grief cloud his belief in God, but his strength and kindness toward her had shown he was a man of faith. She hadn't been sure last night whether she believed in God, not knowing her past, but tonight, in the church service, she'd found her faith again.

She realized Mark had stopped reading. Angelica was curled in his arms, her eyelids heavy.

"It's bedtime, Ange," he said.

"But, Daddy." Her protest was mild. He set her on the floor. "Will you help me put on my new pajamas?"

He brushed his hand over her hair. "Yes, let's see how they look with your cast."

He winked at Serena, and heat rose in her cheeks at the promise in his eyes.

Mark scooped Angelica into his arms and carried her out of the room.

Serena shifted and curled her legs under her. She met Geneva's gaze across the room. "You know who you are now, don't you, my dear?"

"Yes. I thought I would wait until Mark returns and tell you both at the same time, if you don't mind. I won't have to repeat it."

"Mark already knows."

"I realized that, but I can't figure out how he knows. I don't know anyone here in Chicago who could have told him."

Geneva smiled. "I'll let him explain it to you."

Mark walked back into the living room and sat on the sofa, even closer to Serena than earlier. His presence gave her courage.

She took a deep breath. "My name is Serena Cole. That's my maiden name. I was married to Thomas McNeil for five years. We lived in North Carolina." She looked down at her hands. "We had a little girl, Maggie. She was four years old. There was a car accident."

Her voice shook. Mark reached over and covered her hand with his warm, strong one.

She glanced up and saw compassion—and something else—in his eyes. "A pickup truck ran a stoplight and T-boned the driver's side. Tom was killed instantly. Maggie was screaming, and I was in shock. There was blood all over my hands." A sob came out.

"The nightmares," Mark said.

She nodded and wiped the tears from her cheeks. "I couldn't get to her. And by the time the ambulance arrived, the screams had turned to whimpers. Then, they stopped altogether. I had cuts and bruises but no broken bones. My husband's family—they were hateful toward me. They had been from the beginning. I got a business associate's degree after high school. My first job was in the office of their family factory, where Tom was manager. He pursued me—I never really understood why, but he wanted to marry me."

Mark squeezed her hand. "You are very lovable."

"Thank you, but his family didn't think so. My mother was a worker in their factory, and they thought I was beneath Tom. His parents secretly blackmailed me. If I left town, my mother would be able to keep her job and retirement benefits. If I stayed in a relationship with Tom, they would find a reason to terminate her and end her benefits. I left town and started taking classes for a law degree. I thought that was the only way I could free my mother and myself from their blackmail."

"How did you end up marrying Tom, then?" Geneva asked. "Did his parents relent?"

"No. He found out about the blackmail. He never did tell me how. He threatened to go public with it. Instead, they stood back, and we got married. We were happy, at least, in the beginning. We were in love, and despite the odds, I thought we were going to make it. Then, we had Maggie. Tom was of Irish descent, with red hair and green eyes. Maggie had my coloring, and even though she had Tom's eyes, his family objected that she was not Tom's daughter."

"How did your husband feel about that?" Mark looked ready to punch Tom if he found out Tom had turned his back on her.

"He believed me. He always believed in me. Then, after the accident, well, they dragged me through the mud with their accusations. There should have been money from Tom's shares in the family business. He'd left a will. His parents contested it and won. I was left with nothing. I had a settlement from the insurance after the accident, and that kept me afloat. Then, my mother found out she had cancer, and she had to quit her job. She died in November."

"Oh, my dear, I am so sorry," Geneva said. "You have been through so much heartache."

Serena met her gaze. The older woman knew heartache as well. "Yes, but we all have."

Geneva nodded.

Serena released her hand from Mark's grip and stretched it. It had begun to fall asleep from the pressure of his around it. "I thought you could take me back to my hotel tonight so I'll be out of your way."

"You are not in our way." Mark's steady gaze was reassuring.

"I am afraid if you leave tonight, it will break Angelica's heart," Geneva said. "She's so excited to have her Christmas angel here."

"I'm not an angel."

Mark lifted her chin so she could meet his gaze. "You are a hero. You saved Angelica. And you have nowhere else to go, no one who is missing you. If you leave tonight, we'll miss you."

"But I don't belong here."

Geneva got up and left the room. Serena watched her go, then looked back at Mark. He shifted on the sofa so he was facing her. "I disagree, Serena. I feel like you do belong here, with us."

"I'll stay tonight so I'm here for Angelica in the morning. But then, I want you to take me back to my hotel afterward. I have to get ready for the new job I start the day after Christmas."

"About that. There's something you should know. Lily's last name was Miles. She never changed it after we were married. Lily Geneva Miles."

"Lily Gen—" Her heart stopped. "L. G. Miles, attorney at law. That's who I was hired to work for. That's your wife?"

The corners of his mouth tugged upward. "I took over her practice after she passed away. I wanted to leave it in her name, out of respect for her."

She frowned. "But I was interviewed and hired by a woman named Shannon. I thought she was an attorney."

"Shannon is my legal assistant."

It was almost too much to take in. She'd been hired by Mark's assistant. She'd moved from North Carolina to Chicago to start the new job. She'd been walking downtown, shopping, when she stood on the corner beside Geneva and Angelica. The little girl, the one she'd sprinted toward and pushed out of the way of the car, was the daughter of her new employer.

"Some people would say it's a coincidence." Mark took her hands in his. "But I've come to agree with Shannon and with my mother-in-law. I think it was a God thing."

She looked at their joined hands, their left ring fingers showing barely visible white lines. God had brought her here to Chicago. He'd set her in the path of Angelica to save her from injury. Mark had stepped in at the hospital to protect her. He'd brought her to his home. She'd been a stranger to him, and he'd taken care of her anyway.

"So, when did you find out who I was? You knew at the Christmas Eve service—and I hadn't told you yet."

He rubbed her knuckles with his thumbs. "Shannon called tonight before the service and told me she figured out that you were the assistant she hired. She recognized you from the picture we sent."

"We did a video interview. She would have known what I looked like from that."

"When Shannon told me she realized it last night, I asked why she didn't call then, to tell us, to tell you, to see if it jarred your memory free."

How could Shannon have kept such an important piece of information from them? She'd known the missing piece of the puzzle and kept Mark and Serena in the dark. "Why wouldn't she tell me so I could ease my mind?"

"It seems Shannon is a bit of a matchmaker, and apparently, my mother-in-law is, too. Shannon called Geneva last night and told her who you were. They decided to hold off on telling us until Christmas, hoping we might discover feelings for each other." He grinned. "Which I think we did."

Yes. They'd discovered an attraction to each other, which had blossomed into this deep affection and tenderness. The start of something wonderful between them.

Serena withdrew her hands from Mark's. She stifled a laugh. "I should be angry with them, but

I'm not."

"She'll be glad to hear that. She kept telling me I'd like my new assistant. This morning, she had a big grin on her face when she told me that. Now, I know why."

Serena reached up and touched his cheek. "Aren't you angry with Shannon and Geneva for their matchmaking plan?"

"I love Geneva and Shannon both. They only had my best interests in mind. Geneva has tried to set me up so many times, but I've always declined. Now, I know why."

She thought she knew, but she wanted to hear him say it. She brought her hand down and laid her palm against his chest. His heart beat steadily. His gaze was warm and tender, his gold-flecked eyes drawing her in. "I was waiting for you, Serena. I just didn't know it."

She studied him. He was a handsome man with a strong jaw and firm mouth. A mouth that had kissed her and brought her delight. He was a good and loving father and son-in-law. She'd seen him at the church tonight, talking to the people who came up to greet him. He was a man she could admire—and love.

Mark stood, then tugged her to her feet. He wrapped his arms around her waist. "Angelica believed God sent you here in answer to her Christmas wish. She wants a new mommy.

Geneva and Shannon both believe God brought you into our lives as well. That it was no coincidence you stepped in front of the vehicle and rescued Angelica." His smile was gentle. "After tonight, I believe it, too."

He looked so sincere, and joy swelled in her heart. Then, she recalled his response to Angelica's wish. "But you don't want a new wife. You said you don't want to replace Lily."

He hung his head, then looked at her. "I didn't know how special you were when I said that. There was something, right from the start, that drew me to you. I didn't know what it was." He brought his hands up and cupped her cheeks. "Now, I do."

"I'm going to work for you. Won't it be a problem?"

"Not for me. I know you're qualified to do the job. And it will give us time to get to know one another, to see if this connection we have is the lasting kind." His voice was husky. "I love you, Serena."

She bit her lip, staring at the top button on his shirt. He waited. Her arm in its sling was sandwiched between them, but she placed her free hand on his shoulder. As her gaze met his, she was overwhelmed with happiness. But it was a little confusing, the suddenness and depth of her feelings for him.

"I don't know you," she whispered. "How can I love you already? Because I do."

He brushed his lips against hers. "I want you to be in my life—mine and Angelica's—forever."

She toyed with a button on his shirt and sighed as a wave of sadness swept over her. "Sometimes, forever isn't very long. We both lost spouses we loved with all our hearts, that we thought we would grow old with."

He clasped her hand, drew it to his lips, and pressed a kiss against her palm. "I don't understand why it happened or how God works, but I do believe in miracles, especially at Christmastime. You are my Christmas miracle."

She felt it, too. All the grief and sadness that had been in her heart when she came to Chicago had melted away in the discovery of Mark's love. "I'll stay until morning, when Angelica opens her gifts. Then, we can talk about"—she waved her hand between them—"this. Us."

"Fair enough." Mark started to turn away, then hesitated. "May I walk you to your door and kiss you good night, Serena Cole?"

She smiled. "As you wish. We can call this our first date."

"The first of many, I hope."

CHAPTER EIGHTEEN

IT WAS A LONG NIGHT. SERENA could hardly sleep, tossing and turning as thoughts of the past two days ran through her mind. By five o'clock, she gave up on sleep. She got up and followed the smell of coffee to the kitchen. Mark sat at the table, and Geneva was frying sausage to make gravy.

They looked up when she walked in. Geneva's smile was gentle and welcoming. Mark's expression filled her face with heat.

"Good morning, Serena," Geneva said. "How did you sleep?"

"I don't think I did. This is all—overwhelming."

Geneva's eyes twinkled. "Yes, it is. God works in mysterious ways."

Serena walked over to the coffeepot and poured a cup. She stood with her back against the sink, watching Geneva. "I hear you had a part in solving the mystery."

Geneva looked at her out of the corner of her eye. "I'm sorry about withholding your information from you."

"You weren't the only one. I understand that Shannon realized it two nights ago and told you."

A guilty look crossed Geneva's face. "Will you forgive two meddling women?"

Serena laughed. "I will." She peered at the pan of sausage. "Especially since you're making my favorite breakfast."

"It won't be like you have in the South," Geneva said.

Serena laid her hand on Geneva's shoulder. "It will still taste like home."

Mark cleared his throat. Her gaze met his. The love he'd professed last night glowed in his eyes this morning. She walked over to the table and sat around the corner from him. He held a coffee mug in one hand, and she reached for his other hand and covered it with hers. He grinned. She smiled back.

Then, his grin faded. "Are you homesick?"

"No. Funny—I was when I first got to Chicago. That night, I cried when I tried to go to sleep. And it was so cold the next morning. I went shopping for a pair of boots, warm ones I could walk around in."

"I'm afraid your boots were stolen, along with your purse."

"Boots can be replaced."

"Yes, they can. Most things can be replaced." He leaned across the table, close enough for her to kiss him. "It doesn't mean what we had before wasn't wonderful, because it was. You loved your husband, and I loved Lily. But this—between us—is something pretty special."

She smiled around her mug, then set her cup down. He moved the extra few inches and kissed her.

Geneva cleared her throat. "Let's have none of that in my kitchen now." She was smiling, though.

"Daddy! Nana!" Angelica's voice could be heard before they saw her. "Miss Chris!"

"In here, Ange," Mark said.

She came running into the kitchen. Her hair was slipping out of its braids, little wisps everywhere. She had the most joyous smile on her face. "It's Christmas. Santa came!"

Mark slapped his hands against his cheeks. "How do you know?"

Her eyes got round as saucers. "There are presents under the tree. Some of them are for me, right? Please say yes."

He put his arm around her shoulders and drew her to him. "Yes, I'm sure there are some presents under the tree for you."

Her chin dipped. "But not the one I want the most."

Mark put his finger beneath her chin and lifted it so he could look into her sad eyes. "What one did you want the most?" It looked like he knew but wanted her to say it.

"I wanted Miss Chris to become my new mommy."

"There's something we need to talk to you about, Angelica," he said.

Serena laid a hand on his. "Let me." She brushed a wisp of hair from Angelica's cheek. "Angelica, last night, I remembered who I am."

Her eyes widened. "Who are you?"

"My name is Serena Cole."

"That is a pretty name. Se-re-na." Angelica tested it, exaggerating the pronunciation.

Serena smiled. "I'm new to Chicago. I came here to start a job."

"Oh." Angelica grasped Serena's hand that lay across her chest, held in place by the sling. Her eyes filled with tears as her gaze met Serena's. "Do you have to leave us now?"

Serena squeezed her hand. "I have to go to my hotel room today, but I'll come and visit you again soon."

"But why can't you stay with us? You can marry my daddy and sleep in his room. Like Mommy did."

Serena's face heated, and she met Mark's gaze. He was grinning at her. She turned back to Angelica. "I don't know your daddy very well, not well enough to marry him right now. But I do like your daddy very much."

"He likes you very much, too," Mark whispered. He leaned close enough that his breath made her neck tingle.

Angelica turned to him and laid her hands on his knees. She looked from his smiling face to Serena's; then, she giggled. "Maybe you will be my new mommy—someday."

Serena's breath caught in her throat at the light of love in Mark's eyes. Then, she patted Angelica's shoulder. "For now, I'll be your very best friend. How does that sound?"

"Okay. But you have to be Daddy's best friend, too."

Serena smiled. "I think I can do that."

Geneva turned toward them with glad light in her eyes. Serena wondered how Geneva could stand to have Mark marry again, but it was obvious she wished for his and Angelica's happiness. Serena felt so blessed to have this woman welcome her into her family, even though nothing was official yet.

"The sausage gravy and biscuits are done. Are you all ready to eat?"

Angelica crossed her arms. "No, I want to

open presents first."

Mark shook his head. "You might not remember, but we always eat breakfast first on Christmas morning."

She pouted. "Why?"

"Because if we don't, then you don't eat because you're playing with your new things." He pulled out her chair and motioned for her to sit down.

"Okay. I want to say the prayer." After everything was set on the table, Angelica looked around at them all. She bowed her head and folded her hands. "Dear God in Heaven, thank You that it's Christmas. Thank You for the presents. For Miss Chris—I mean, Se-re-na—who had nam-neesha, but now she doesn't. I hope she can be my mommy someday"—she paused dramatically—"but I'm glad she is going to be my best friend. And thank You that she is going to be Daddy's best friend, too. Amen."

They raised their heads and opened their eyes. She looked around, then quickly closed her eyes again. "And thank You for this food. Amen."

It was the sweetest prayer Serena had heard since she listened to Maggie's bedtime prayers. Sadness spilled into her heart at the bittersweet memories. A little girl, loved so much, gone too fast from this life. And another little girl, motherless, looking for someone to love her. God had certainly brought them full circle.

She ate a few bites of her biscuits and gravy. "Geneva, these biscuits are so delicious and light, and the gravy is amazing."

Geneva dropped her gaze, but her cheeks reddened, and it was obvious she took pleasure in Serena's words. "Coming from you, Serena, I'll take that as a compliment. Since you are an expert on the subject."

Serena smiled. "Not an expert, maybe. But I don't think you need any instruction. These have the down-home goodness I've been craving."

Angelica tried to rush them through the meal, so they finally gave up eating and went into the living room with her. She ran to the tree and knelt in front of it. She squealed when she read her name out loud.

"Are they all for you?" Mark asked.

"No. Of course not. But a lot of them are!" She picked up a present and held it to her chest.

"Why don't you pass them all out?" he suggested. "Then, we can watch you open them."

It took a few minutes for Angelica to read the names on the packages and pass them out. She struggled with the word on some of the packages. "What is G-U-E-S-T?"

"That spells *guest*," Mark said.

"Oh, yeah. Those are the gifts for Miss Chris— oops." Angelica covered her mouth with her hand.

"I forgot. Serena."

"There are gifts for me?" Serena was shocked to be included. Angelica carried one over to her. Serena's eyes went to Geneva. "You didn't have to get me anything."

"Mark suggested it."

Serena raised her eyebrows as she stared at Mark. "How did you know I would be staying until this morning?"

He grinned. "I didn't, but I guess, even then, I was hoping that you'd be with us for a few days."

When all the presents were passed out, Angelica sat on the floor, surrounded by her gifts. The adults watched as she tore open the wrappings, like the six-year-old she was.

"A baby doll, like the one I saw in the commercial." She held up the humanlike doll dressed in a pink sleeper and pressed a button on her hand. The baby doll said, "Mama."

"Thank you; thank you; thank you!" Angelica tore open another one, and it was a plastic tea set with princesses on the pieces. "I can play tea party!" She grinned at Serena. "You can come to my party, Serena."

"I'd like that," Serena said, meaning it. She hoped that in the coming days, she'd be able to spend a lot of time with Angelica. It didn't mean she would never miss Maggie and Tom again. She would always carry their memories in her heart, but she had room to start new memories with Mark and his family.

Angelica opened a big box and found a pair of white ice skates with pink laces. "Oh, these are bea-u-ti-ful, Daddy and Nana. I can't wait to go ice-skating."

Mark chuckled. "You'll have to wait, for at least six weeks, remember, Angelica? The doctor said you won't be able to skate until your cast comes off." He met Geneva's gaze. "Remind me to look up that number for the orthopedic doctor. I'll call tomorrow morning and see when I can get an appointment for her." Then, his gaze turned to Serena. "We also need to call the police station and get the insurance information of the driver so we can get your hospital bills paid."

"Let's not talk about all of that today," Serena said, laying her hand on his. "We have plenty of time to take care of those things tomorrow."

Tomorrow, they would be at the office, together, getting acquainted in their new roles as employer and employee. And she would meet Shannon, whose matchmaking plot had turned out perfectly well.

Angelica finished unwrapping her gifts. She stood and waded through the paper to hug Geneva, then Mark. She hugged Serena, too.

"I'm sorry I didn't get anything for you, Angelica. I wasn't expecting to celebrate

Christmas with anyone."

"That's okay. You can buy me something later."

Her offhand comment made the adults laugh, and Angelica looked confused.

She placed a package in Serena's hands. "Now, you open yours."

"Your daddy and Nana should go first."

"But I can't wait for you to see what I bought for you."

"Go ahead," Mark said. Geneva nodded.

Serena opened the present. It was a bottle of perfume.

"That's from Daddy," Angelica said.

Mark blushed. "What can I say? I'm so cliché."

"I like this kind."

Angelica set the large gift in front of Serena. It held a stylish purse in a forest-green color she loved so much.

"It's from Nana, because you lost yours when you saved me."

Serena smiled. "Thank you, Geneva. It is one of my favorite colors."

"I took a guess, and I'm glad you like it."

Lastly, Angelica handed her a gift that looked about the size and shape of a candle. Serena opened it carefully, thinking about how she should make her response extra enthusiastic. But when she opened the box, she found a carved figurine. It didn't have a face painted on it, but it wasn't hard to tell that it was an angel standing behind a little girl. The angel's hands were on the child's shoulders.

"Oh, Angelica. It's lovely. So precious." Serena held it in one hand and wrapped her other arm around Angelica's shoulders. "But you know I'm not really an angel, right?"

"Right. But I can still call you that because you saved me."

Mark put his arm around Serena's shoulders. "And you saved me."

She frowned. "How did I save you?"

"I was stuck in the past. I tried to move on, but I was still angry with God for Lily and the baby's deaths." He brushed a curl back from her cheek. "And then, I met you, and you were all goodness and light."

Angelica placed her hand on Serena's knee and smiled up at her. "See—you're Daddy's angel, too."

Serena reached for Angelica's hand, and Mark wrapped both of theirs in his. "I think it's the two of you who saved me," Serena said. "I was lost when I came to Chicago. I, too, was stuck in my past. Finding you, even though it was through strange circumstances, that pain is gone from my heart."

Geneva cleared her throat. "I think it's time

Angelica and I go and get dressed."

"But, Nana."

Geneva stood and held out her hand. "Come, Angelica." Angelica reluctantly let go of Serena's hand and stormed across the room. She followed Geneva down the hallway.

Serena still held Mark's hand, and he entwined their fingers. The tenderness in his eyes made her catch her breath.

"Serena, I know we just met—and through odd circumstances. Shannon and Geneva may have done a little matchmaking, but God is the one who ultimately brought you to Chicago and literally set you in the path of my family. I believe He brought you here to be my wife."

Heat filled her cheeks as she thought about what it would mean to become Mark's wife. Not only would she have the love of this amazing man; she would also have the blessings of a delightful child and a mother in Geneva. She already loved them.

Mark moved his hands to her shoulders. "We need time to get to know one another, and we'll do that as we work together. But today, Serena, I give you my heart. A heart free of grief and pain and ready to love again."

"And I give you mine."

As their lips met in a kiss that promised forever, Serena knew she would always remember the Christmas when she lost her identity and found a new place to belong.

ABOUT THE AUTHOR

CAROL UNDERHILL lives in a small village in rural Michigan. She is mom to three adult children and a spoiled black Lab. Her household also includes several rescued cats. She likes hazelnut coffee, finding new authors and binge-reading their books, and has a music playlist for every mood.

You can follow her writing journey:
Facebook:
www.facebook.com/authorcarolunderhill
Twitter: @underhill7
Website: www.authorcarolunderhill.com
www.anaiahpress.com

Made in the USA
Lexington, KY
03 December 2019